AEM

Diana Palmer has published over seventy category romances, as well as historical romances and longer contemporary works. With over forty million copies of her books in print, Diana Palmer is one of North America's most beloved authors. Her accolades include two *Romantic Times* Reviewer's Choice Awards, a Maggie Award, five national Waldenbooks bestseller awards and two national B. Dalton bestseller awards. Diana resides in the north mountains of her home state of Georgia with her husband, James, and their son, Blayne Edward.

Sweet Enemy

DIANA PALMER

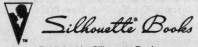

Published by Silhouette Books

America's Publisher of Contemporary Romance

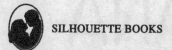 SILHOUETTE BOOKS

ISBN 0-373-51206-6

SWEET ENEMY

First published in North America as a MacFadden Romance by Kim Publishing Corporation.

Copyright © 1979 by Diana Palmer.

Visit Silhouette at www.eHarlequin.com

Printed In U.S.A.

One

"**I** won't go!" Maggie Kirk said stubbornly, and turned away from her friend's cajoling pleas. "It's like asking me to walk into a Bengal tiger's cage with a sirloin roast tied around my neck!"

"But, Maggie," Janna protested, her dark eyes pleading softly, "it's just what you need. Remember how we used to escape to the ranch when we were in school, how we looked forward to riding and picnicking by the river?"

"My memories are a little different," the slender brunette said with a grimace. She perched on the edge of the bed, studying the legs of her brown denim jeans. "I remember being put over Clint Raygen's knee for riding that surly stallion of his, and being locked in my room for going on a picnic by the river with Gerry Broome."

"Clint did warn you about High Tide," her small friend reminded her, defending the brother she worshipped. "And you know what Gerry tried to do. Clint knew he was too old to trust you with."

Maggie blushed with the memory of Clint finding her fighting her way out of Gerry's furious embrace, and the sight of blood when his big fist connected with the younger man's nose. The lecture that followed hadn't been pleasant, either. She sighed. It had always been like that. She and Clint had been enemies from their first encounter, when she was eight and he was nineteen and she threw a baseball bat at him.

"It was a long time ago," Janna reminded her. "You're twenty now, and it was all right when we went down to spend a week with Clint and Mama last summer, wasn't it?"

"Of course it was all right, he was in Europe!" Maggie erupted. "This time, your mother's in Europe, and Clint's home, and Lida's just dumped him and he's going to be an absolute pain in the neck!"

"That's why I think you should go," Janna said.

Maggie gaped at her. "Janna, old friend, have you been tippling the brandy bottle again?"

"Well, here you are just getting over that rat, Philip," Janna explained, "and there he is just getting over that ratess, Lida..."

"Haven't you ever noticed that although your brother and I are probably very nice people when we're separated, we seem to turn rabid when we come face to face?"

Maggie asked patiently. "The last time," she reminded the wide-eyed girl, "he threw me, fully clothed, into the river, I hit my...my embarrassment on a rock," she faltered.

"You kicked him," Janna replied. "Hard. On the shin."

"He called me an idiot!"

"Well, what would you call somebody who tried to stone a rattlesnake to death from four feet?" Janna threw up her hands. "Honestly, Maggie, when you get around my brother, you lose every ounce of sense you have."

"There you go again... Oh, never mind." She propped her chin on her elbows. "It's no use talking about it, anyway. Clint won't have me down to the ranch without you, and we both know it."

"Yes, he will. I asked him."

"What did you tell him?" Maggie asked suspiciously, her emerald eyes sparkling.

Janna shrugged. "That you and Phil had split, that's all."

"Just that…not how we broke up?" she asked quietly.

"I swear, Maggie. I'd never do that to you."

She forced a wan smile. "I didn't mean that. It…I guess it hit me a little harder than I expected."

"Clint said you could fill in for his secretary while she's on vacation," Janna continued brightly, "and have a working holiday that you'll get paid for. He said it would be the best medicine you'd ever swallowed."

"And, knowing Clint, he'll add a teaspoon of arsenic just to flavor it," Maggie grumbled. "Arrogant, hard headed, bossy…"

"You are between jobs," Janna reminded her.

Maggie sighed. "If I were drowning, you'd toss me an anchor, wouldn't you, my bosom buddy?"

"Oh, Maggie, it's a golden opportunity I'm giving you. Three weeks with the most eligible bachelor in the Sunshine State, good-looking, rich, desirable..."

"I think I'm going to be sick," Maggie said, turning her gaze to the budding trees outside the window.

"Haven't you ever had a romantic thought about Clint, in all these years?" Janna persisted.

"Sorry to disappoint you, but, no."

"The best cure for a broken heart is to get it broken again."

"Golly, gee, Janna, look at the pretty bird on the limb here," Maggie said enthusiastically. "Isn't he just too gorgeous?"

"Okay, okay. Will you at least go to the ranch?"

"Next to hell, it's my very favorite place when Clint's there."

"It's pretty on the ranch right now—all the wildflowers are in bloom." Janna sighed. "Clint's always out on the range somewhere, with the cattle or the field hands, and you know he almost never gets to the house before dark.''

''And there's always hope that he'll get captured by rustlers and held for ransom until my vacation's over, right?'' Maggie grinned.

''Right!'' Janna laughed.

Maggie was never really certain why she decided to take the bus. Perhaps it was because so many pleasant memories of her childhood were connected with it, when she had ridden from her parents' home in Atlanta to her grandparents' home in South Georgia on the big, comfortable bus. And from there, it was just a pleasant drive to Janna and Clint's family's ranch in Florida.

Maggie's eyes were drawn to that long, level landscape, where pine trees, pecan orchards, and spacious farm houses stood sheltering under the towering oaks and chinaberry trees. Her childhood had been spent here, riding over these fields on horseback with Janna. Usually Clint was in hot pursuit while she bent low over the horse's neck. The wind would cut into her face as she urged her mount on, after flinging back a challenge to Clint. The tall man's eyes always had a pale green glint to them when she challenged him, and he always gave her just enough rope to hang herself.

She smiled involuntarily at the memory. She and Clint had never actually decided on the boundaries of their relationship. The banter between them was usually friendly, although it could get hot. But it had never been really malicious or cruel. They were the eternal odd couple, always rubbing each other wrong, always wary around each other as if they held an uneasy truce and were afraid it might fall and break.

Clint was too rugged to ever be called handsome, but he drew women. He always had them hanging on his arm, and Maggie was determined from the beginning never to be one of those poor moths drawn to his flame. She resisted his charm effortlessly, because he never wasted it on her, and she was glad. She'd never been completely sure how she'd react to Clint in that kind of relationship. Because she was afraid of it, she worked minor miracles to prevent it from ever happening.

A buzz of conversation caught her attention, and she drew herself back to the present just in time to see the people across the aisle staring fixedly out the window. The bus slowly ground to a halt as a rider came straight toward it on a black stallion that gleamed like silk in the sun.

Maggie didn't have to be told who was riding the horse. The man's tall, easy arrogance was a dead giveaway, even without the cocky angle of his range hat and the khaki work clothes that seemed to be a part of him.

He reined up at the door as the bus driver opened it with a grin.

"Man, can you ride," he laughed, shaking his curly dark head appreciatively.

"I've had my share of practice," Clint Raygen said with a lopsided smile. His dancing green eyes found Maggie moving up to the front of the bus in her powder blue pantsuit and he raised a lazy eyebrow at her.

"Thank God you're still tomboy enough to wear pants, Irish," he said, throwing down the gauntlet effortlessly with that hated nickname from her childhood. "I don't have time to meet the bus. We're tagging some new cattle. Hop on."

"Hop...on?" she echoed weakly. "But...my luggage?"

"The driver can drop it off in town, can't you?" he asked the man. "We'll get it later."

"I'll do it," the driver said, "on condition if I ever get two days in a row, you'll teach me to ride a horse like that."

"I own the C bar R," Clint told him.

"You're welcome anytime. Maggie, hop aboard."

There was a muffled giggle from behind her, and she didn't have to turn to know it was a couple of teenagers who were in the seat behind hers. She straightened her shoulders. There was no way out of this, for sure, not without becoming the object of everybody's conversation for the rest of the way into town.

"I haven't been on a horse in a year," she told him, as she took the lean, brown hand he held out.

"Step up on my boot and swing your leg over," he said in his best you-Jane-me-Tarzan voice, and she could almost see the teenagers swooning.

She managed to get herself up behind him without too much effort, but it was a disturbing new contact, and she had to hold on tight to his hard waist to keep from sliding off the big horse. It was like digging her fingers into solid steel, those whipcord muscles were so powerful.

"All set, Maggie?" he asked over his shoulder.

"All set," she murmured in a low voice that wouldn't carry farther than his ear. "Ready to gallop away in a cloud of dust and leave your adoring public gasping in the wake of your dramatic exit!"

She felt his chest shake under her hand as he urged the stallion into a slow canter and headed out across the field.

"If this isn't dramatic enough for you, Irish," he said arrogantly, "I'll put Whirlwind into a gallop."

Both slender arms went around him and she held on for all she was worth. "Oh, please don't, Clint, I'll be good," she said quickly.

He chuckled deeply. "I thought you would. I'll drop you by the house on my way to the feedlot."

"You sure picked an unusual way to meet me," she remarked, watching the high grass wave along the path the horse was making.

"I didn't plan it," he said casually. "I just happened to see the bus, and I figured you'd be on it."

She wondered at that. Clint always seemed to know when she was coming. He always had. It was as if he had a built-in radar where she was concerned.

She stared at that broad, unyielding back. "Thank you for letting me come," she said quietly.

"Janna said you needed a job," he replied matter-of-factly. "And I happen to be between secretaries," he added in a taut voice. It went without saying that Lida had been the last one.

She turned her attention to the long horizon, dotted with pine trees and scrub palmettos and red-coated Herefords with their faces tiny dots of white in the distance. Involuntarily, a smile came to her face.

"Janna and I used to play cowboys and Indians in those fields," she murmured. "I always had to be the Indian."

He glanced down at her leg in the loose

slacks. "You still dress like one," he said. "I've hardly ever seen you in a dress, Irish."

She shifted restlessly. "They're a little out of place on a farm, don't you think?" she grumbled. It was the old argument again, he never tired of chiding her about her preference for slacks.

"I hadn't planned on using you to tag cattle and bale hay," he growled.

She drew a sharp, angry breath. "How I dress is my business," she replied. "All you have to worry about is if I can type and take dictation."

He reined in abruptly and half-turned in the saddle, twisting his tall body so that he could look back at her. His narrowed eyes were a menacing pale green.

"I'll remind you once that there's a line you don't cross with me, little girl," he said in a soft tone that cut more surely than shouting would have. "Your whipped pup of a boyfriend may have taken backtalk with a grin, but don't expect the same consideration from me. I still say a woman's got only one use to a man, and I think you know what I'm talking about.''

She did, and nothing could have prevented the blush that colored her high cheekbones. She looked away quickly.

He studied her quietly, his eyes tracing the delicate profile turned toward him. ''Why do you screw your hair up like that?'' he asked suddenly.

She gritted her teeth. ''It keeps it out of my eyes,'' she replied tightly.

''And keeps a man's eyes turned the other way,'' he added. ''How did that city dude ever get through the layer of ice around you, Irish? With a blowtorch?''

That brought her emerald eyes flashing around to burn into his. ''Would you rather I'd have come in a slinky, skin-tight dress with my face plastered in makeup, batting my eyelashes at you?'' she asked hotly.

His bold, slow eyes ran over her face, down to her soft mouth, further down to the full, young curves of her body. "You did that once," he recalled gently, meeting her shocked, uncertain gaze. "When you were seventeen, and I suddenly became the star in your young sky after Gerry Broome threw you over."

The memory was like an open wound. He'd never let her forget it. She couldn't forget, either, how she'd run after him shamelessly, finding excuse after excuse to follow him around the ranch that unforgettable summer. Until finally he'd gotten tired of it and shattered her pride into a thousand aching pieces by confronting her with the crush, a confrontation that had shamed her into hiding. She'd never quite recovered from the rejection, keeping it buried in her subconscious. It was one reason she fought him so hard, keeping anger like a safe, high fence between them.

She dropped her eyes to the broad chest in front of her. "That was three years ago," she said quietly.

"And now there's Philip," he added.

There was a note in his deep, slow voice that defied analysis. "Isn't there?"

She clenched her jaw. "No," she whispered achingly, "there isn't. Didn't Janna tell you that we'd split?"

His eyes narrowed. "My sister doesn't tell me a damned thing. So you threw him over, Irish?"

She met that taunting gaze levelly. "I caught him with one of my bridesmaids after the rehearsal," she told him, "going into a motel room together."

He studied her thoughtfully. "Were you that cold, that he had to find another woman to warm him?"

She flinched. "Damn you!" she breathed. "I might have expected that you'd see anybody's side of it except mine. It's always been that way with us."

"It's always going to be that way," he said quietly, something deep and strange in the eyes that searched hers, "because you don't want me on your side. You want a damned wall between us for some reason. What the hell are you afraid of?''

"You can ask me that, with your reputation?'' she scoffed.

A slow, mocking smile touched his cruel mouth. "Little girl, you flatter yourself. Even forgetting the fact that I could give you eleven years, you don't stir me in a physical sense, Maggie. You never have.'' His eyes swept along her boyish figure. "It would be like making love to a snow sculpture.''

She kept her face cool. It would never do to let him know how much he could hurt her. "I thought I came here to be your secretary, not your whipping boy,'' she said coolly. "Or do you expect me to pay for Lida's sins, along with my own?''

She saw his eyes narrow, the muscles in his jaw moving ominously. "My God, you're asking for it,'' he warned softly.

She straightened, moving as far away from him as it was possible to move on horseback. "You started it!''

"I can finish it, too," he said curtly.

She looked away. "I told Janna it wouldn't work," she bit off. "If you'll kindly take me to the house, I'll get a cab back to the bus station."

"Running away, Irish?" he growled. "You're good at that."

Her lower lip trembled. "I won't be crucified by you!" she burst out on a sob. "Oh, God, I hate men, I hate men," she whispered. "Cheats and liars, all of you!"

His lean hand caught the nape of her neck and drew her forehead against his broad shoulder, as he twisted further in the saddle. "How many women were there before you found out?" he asked at her ear.

A sob shook her. "Four, five; I lost count," she whispered. "We were going to be married just two days after...he said I wouldn't melt in a...in a blast furnace," her voice broke again. Her small hand curled against the warm muscles of his arm. "And he...he was right. I didn't feel that way with him, I couldn't...!'' She drew a long, sobbing breath.

His fingers tightened on her slender neck. "How old was he?" he asked gently.

She swallowed down another sob. "Twenty-seven."

"Experienced?"

"Very."

"Was he patient, Maggie?" he asked.

She drew a soft breath, her eyes closing tightly. "He...took it for granted that I knew...well, that I..."

His chest rose deeply against her, and fell with a sound like impatience. "It's just as well, Irish," he said at her ear. "Better to find him out now than after the wedding."

"Clint, I'm sorry I jumped..." she began.

His cheek moved against hers, rough and warm. "Dry up, little watering pot. I've got cattle to tend, and Emma's going to be standing on her head wondering what happened to us. Okay now?''

''Yes.'' She managed a wan smile for him. ''Clint, I'm sorry about Lida...''

His face was shuttered, but not angry. He flicked a careless forefinger against her nose. ''Let's go home.''

He turned back to the saddle horn and coaxed the stallion into a canter. He didn't say another word until they got to the sprawling white frame ranch house in its nest of oaks and pecan trees. He let her down at the white fence beside the front porch.

Sitting astride the black stallion, he was an impressive figure, tall in the saddle and ramrod straight. He lit a cigarette, his eyes studying her quietly for a long moment.

''Must you stare at me like that?'' she asked uneasily, shifting under the bold thoroughness of his scrutiny. ''I feel like a heifer on market day.''

Something cruel flashed in his pale eyes. ''I'm not putting in any bids,'' he replied innocently. "I'll have one of the boys fetch your luggage. Emma'll get you something to eat. I'll explain what I need done when I get in tonight."

The coldness in him, so sudden and unexpected, made chills run down her spine. For years they'd been make-believe enemies. But this felt like the real thing. He looked at her as if…as if he hated her!

"I still think it might be better if I went home," she said.

"You'll stick it out," he countered sharply. "I can't get a replacement at this short notice, and I've got correspondence backed up to the eaves, with a sale day coming up."

"Orders, Mr. Raygen?" she fumed.

A wisp of a smile touched that hard, stern face that was so much a stranger's, emphasizing the nose that had been broken at least twice and showed it. "Orders, Irish."

"Will you stop calling me that? You know I hate it!"

"By all means, hate it. Hate me, too, if it helps. I don't give a damn, and you know that, too, don't you, little girl?" he asked with a hellish grin.

She whirled on her heels and stalked through the gate onto the long white porch, with its rocking chairs and wide porch swing and pots filled with blooming flowers.

Two

Emma was rolling out dough in the spacious, homey kitchen when Maggie walked in and, unmindful of the flour up to her elbows, she grabbed the younger woman in a bearish hug.

Maggie laughed, smothered in the ample girth of Emma's huge embrace, feeling really at home for the first time.

"It's so good to have another woman here, I could jump for joy," Emma grinned, running one floury hand through her short, silver hair. "Clint Raygen's been like a wild man for the past month. I'll swear, I never thought a hussy like that Lida Palmes could affect him in such a way. If you ask me, it's just hurt pride that's eating him, but it doesn't make any difference to his temper."

"So I've noticed," Maggie sighed, and sat down at the long kitchen table where Emma was making bread. "What did she do to him?"

"Walked out on him without a word. Not even a day's notice." She shrugged. "Found herself a rich Florida millionaire, they said."

"He couldn't have been that much richer than Clint," Maggie remarked.

"He wasn't," Emma smiled. "And he had twenty years on him, to boot. Nobody understood what got into her. One day she was queening it over me and the ranch hands, the next she was gone."

"Was it very long ago?" she asked idly.

"Let's see—hard to remember things at my age, you know. But...oh, yes, it was the day Janna called to tell us we were invited to your wedding." She laughed. "We didn't even know you were engaged, you secretive little thing."

Maggie's eyes fell. "I guess you knew we called off the wedding."

Emma's floured hand touched hers gently. "It's for the best. We both know that, don't we?"

She nodded with a misty smile. "I wasn't desperately in love with him, but I did like him a lot. I guess my pride's hurt, too."

"You'll get over it. When one door closes, another opens, Maggie, my dear."

"You're right, of course," she managed cheerfully. "Janna sends her love. She said she'll try to get her vacation early and come on down in a few weeks."

"That would be nice, to have both of you home for a while. Well," she said, kneading dough rhythmically, "tell me all the latest news."

It was well after dark, and Emma and Maggie were just getting everything on the dining room table when Clint came striding in the front door. His jeans were red with mud, his shirt wet with sweat, his jaw showing a shadow of a beard. He barely spared them a glance before he went down the long hall that led to his room.

"Whiskey," Emma remarked with a nod, and poured a glass two inches deep of the amber liquid before adding a touch of water and two ice cubes to it. "I can tell by his walk."

"Tell what?" Maggie asked.

"What kind of day it's been. The cattle must have given him fits."

"Not the cattle," Maggie replied wearily. "Me. We got into it on the way home. I should never have come, Emma. It's just like old times."

"Is it, now?" the older woman asked

curiously. "Maybe. And maybe not. We'll see."

Clint came back looking cooler, his dark hair damp from a shower, his face shaven, the work khakis exchanged for a pair of sand-colored slacks and a beige patterned shirt that clung to his muscular arms and chest like a second skin.

His green eyes slid down Maggie's slender figure in pale yellow slacks and a tank top, moving back up to rest narrowly on the familiar bun.

"Welcome back, tomboy," he said with thinly veiled sarcasm.

"Thanks," she replied sweetly. "Emma poured you a drink."

He turned away, found it on the table and threw down a large swallow of it. "Well, sit down," he growled at her, "or do you plan to eat standing up?"

She dragged out a chair and plopped down in it, pointedly avoiding his gaze as Emma brought the rest of the food and finally sat down herself across from Maggie.

"Do I get combat pay?" Emma asked Clint when she caught the icy glares that were being exchanged.

"Put on your armour and shut up," Clint replied, but there was a glint of humor in his tone, and in his pale eyes.

Emma glanced at Maggie with a grin. "Welcome home, honey."

Dinner was pleasant enough after that, but when the last of the coffee was gone, Clint motioned Maggie to follow him, and led her into the darkly masculine den with its gun cabinet and oak desk and deer head mounted over the mantel.

"Get a pencil," he told Maggie. "You'll find one on the desk."

She picked one up out of a pen holder, and borrowed one of the empty legal pads as well before she sat down in the chair beside his big desk.

He turned, his eyes studying her quietly, angrily, for a long moment before he spoke. "How old are you now?" he asked unexpectedly.

"Twenty," she replied quietly.

"Twenty." He lit a cigarette, but his eyes never left her. "Twenty, and still unawakened."

She felt the color rush into her face, and hated it, hated him.

"You're sure about that?" she asked hotly.

He held her eyes for a long time. "I'm very sure, honey," he said softly.

Unable to hold the penetrating gaze for another instant, she dragged her eyes down to the blank sheet of yellow paper and concentrated on the bluish lines that ruled it.

"I thought you wanted to dictate some letters," she said in a tight voice.

"You don't know what I want, little girl," he replied. "And if you did, it would probably scare the hell out of you. Got your pencil ready? Here goes…"

He was dictating before she had time to puzzle out that cryptic remark.

The first few days went by in a rush, and Maggie fell into an easy routine. Clint left the correspondence on her desk every morning, all outlined, so that she could work at her own pace. At night, he signed the letters and checked the records she typed for him, and they both worked at holding their tempers.

She finished early the fifth day and couldn't resist the temptation to go for a ride. Clint had given her a gentle little bay mare for her seventeenth birthday and it was still her favorite mount. Melody was the name she gave it, because of the horse's easy rocking motion as she walked; like a blues melody.

It stirred her emotions to revisit the haunts of her childhood on the large, sprawling farm. Near the tall line of pine trees was the aging, majestic pecan tree that she and Janna climbed long ago— their dreaming tree. Then a little farther along was the thicket where dogwoods grew virgin white in the spring and little girls could gather armloads of them to dream over.

Then, too, there was the river. Maggie reined in the mare and leaned over the saddle horn to watch it flowing lazily like a silver and white ribbon through the trees. The river, where they waded and swam, and where Clint had hurled her—fully clothed—the day she kicked him.

She couldn't resist that cool, inviting water in the heat that was thick and smothering even in the shade of the hardwoods on the bank. She tied Melody to a sapling and tugged off her boots and thick socks.

The water was icy to her bare feet, the river rocks smooth and slippery. She wobbled cautiously near the bank, grabbing onto a low-hanging limb of the bulky oak tree to keep her balance.

With a sigh, she closed her eyes and listened to the watery whisper of the river, the sound of birds calling and moving the leaves over her head as they jumped from bough to bough. The peace she felt was indescribable. It was as if she'd come home. Home.

She remembered Clint's mother baking biscuits in the oven, laughing as she teased Maggie about her pigtails. And Clint, maddening even that long ago, swinging her off the floor in his hard arms to welcome her when she got off the bus at the station. Twelve years ago. A lifetime ago.

She opened her eyes and followed the path of the river downstream with an unseeing blankness in her stare. It was hard to say just when she and Clint had lost that rapport. When she was fourteen—fifteen? There had always been pretend arguments, but as she reached the middle of her teens they had suddenly become real. Clint seemed to provoke them deliberately, as if sparking her hot temper were important, to keep her at a distance. It had been even worse in her seventeenth summer...

She blotted out the thought. As long as she lived, she'd never get over that humiliation. To an already withdrawn teenager, the effect had been devastating. Not until Philip came along had she even tried to open her heart again. Only to have him shatter her pride to tiny bits.

A strand of her hair tumbled into her eyes and rather than try to put it up again, she removed all the pins from her hair and stuck them in her pocket, letting the rich black waves fall gently around her shoulders. It had been a long time since she'd worn her hair down like this outside the privacy of her bedroom. That, too, dated back to Clint's cruelty.

He made no secret of his fondness for long hair, and Maggie had let hers grow to her waist in the months before that summer vacation. She'd even shed her favorite slacks outfits for some frilly sundresses and dainty sandals, all in the hopes of catching Clint's eye. But all she'd caught was Gerry Broome's, and Clint had come to the rescue just in time. Gerry couldn't get away from her fast enough, and Clint always thought that was the reason for her one-woman campaign to reel in his heart. But none of it had worked.

"Save your schemes for a boy your own age, little girl," he'd warned her venomously after a lecture that her cheeks still reddened from three years later. "I want more than long hair and doe eyes when I take a woman in my arms. The only thing about me that you arouse is my temper. I don't want you, Maggie."

The words echoed in her mind for days afterwards, even when she got back home and was caught up in her father's lingering illness and her mother's grief. She'd cut her hair then, and even when it grew again, she kept it tightly capped in the bun. It hadn't come down even for Philip, who loved long hair himself, but wasn't persuasive enough.

With a sigh she sank down on a big boulder at the river's edge, trailing her bare toes through the cold, rippling water, her hair hiding her face from view as she relived the memories.

"Sunning yourself, mermaid?" a taunting voice asked from close behind her.

She whirled with a gasp, almost unseating herself into the stream as she faced Clint. He was leaning carelessly against the trunk of the tree, one dusty boot propped on a chunky root, his forearms crossed over his knee—just watching her. His stallion nibbled at leaves on the oak tree nearby.

"You move...like wind," she accused breathlessly, smoothing the hair away from her face.

"An old hunter's trick. Your mind was far away, little one," he said gently, his eyes sketching her face in its frame of waving black hair.

"I guess it was." She turned back, automatically winding her hair into a braid so that she could pin it up.

"Leave it!" he said, in a tone like a whiplash.

She stiffened with her hands up against

her nape. "It...gets in my way," she said tightly.

"We both know that isn't why."

"You flatter yourself if you think you're the cause of it," she said with practiced calm, reaching into her pocket for some bobby pins. "I'm not seventeen any more, Clint. I'm not vulnerable anymore."

He was behind her before she realized it, arrogantly sweeping the pins from her hand. He jerked her up by the elbows and held her on her tiptoes in the cool, rushing water.

His green eyes narrowed, darkened, as he looked down into her frightened face. It wasn't Clint's familiar, taunting eyes that looked down into hers. He was a stranger—unsmiling, somber, studying her with an intensity that rippled along her nerves.

"Was that a dig, Maggie?" he asked gruffly. "Or did you think I'd forgotten what happened?"

She averted her face and tried not to feel

the steely excitement his fingers were causing. "It was a long time ago," she said as calmly as she could with her heart beating wildly.

"And you're all grown up now, is that it?" He pulled her close against his tall, lean body. "How grown up are you, little girl?" he whispered, and she felt his breath, smoky and warm, whipping across her face.

She pulled furiously against his merciless grip, fighting him for all she was worth. "Let go of me!" she flashed, her loosened hair flying as she twisted against his hands.

"Irish," he taunted softly, holding her easily in spite of her flailing efforts to resist him. "As Irish as a shamrock. Calm down, little tigress, I'm not going to force anything on you."

She did calm down, but more because of her own fatigue than the soothing words. "You beast," she muttered, glaring up at him out of eyes like an angry cat's.

His hands slid up her arms to her throat, holding her flushed young face up to his, and all expression seemed to go out of his own face, leaving his eyes narrow and dark as they looked deep into hers.

"Fire in you," he said gently. "Soft flames, Irish, that could burn a man alive. Did Philip ever see that white-hot temper?"

The intensity of his gaze confused her, shook her. "He didn't know I had a temper," she said unsteadily. Her eyes narrowed, temper coming to her rescue. "You wouldn't know I had one, either, if you'd stop picking on me!"

"I like it when you fight me," he said softly.

She looked up in time to see the light in his leaf-green eyes flare up with the words, and a ghost of a smile touched his hard, chiseled mouth. It was like no look he'd ever given her before—appraising, calculating—almost sensuous. It made her heart tremble, because the way he said it conjured up a picture of a woman fighting the crush of a man's hard arms, the sting of his mouth...

She dropped her eyes to his chest, and suddenly he released her, moving away to light a cigarette with long, steady fingers.

She rubbed her chafed arms. "If...if you want those records typed today, I'd better get back to the house," she said, turning toward the bank. "And," she threw over her shoulder as she bent to wipe her wet feet with a handkerchief, "you owe me a package of bobby pins."

She felt his eyes running over her as she pulled on her boots.

"Leave it down, Irish," he said carelessly, his eyes never leaving her as she got up and untied Melody's reins. "I won't make any more remarks about it, but leave it loose."

She gaped at him, puzzled at the anger in his deep voice—anger that was meant more for himself than for her. With a shrug, she mounted and rode away without a backward glance.

He stood and watched her until she was out of sight, his eyes narrowed against the sun, his face thoughtful and solemn.

Three

Emma only set two places at the supper table, noting Maggie's puzzled glance with a smile.

"Clint's got a date," she explained, leaving Maggie to put the silverware at the places while she went out to the kitchen to bring the food in.

A pain like being shot went through Maggie's slender body, and she wondered at it. For all that her pride had been crushed by Philip, her heart had never been touched by any man—except one. She hated the rush of feeling, the green surge of jealousy that thinking about Clint and a woman, any woman, could cause. It had always been that way, always. And she managed to keep it hidden because of what he'd already done to her stubborn spirit. But it was still there, inside, glowing and sweetly burning like a candle no amount of wind could blow out. And she hated Clint for causing it.

He came in from the feedlot just as Emma and Maggie were finishing up the dishes, and to avoid him, Maggie retreated to the front porch and glued her lean body onto the porch swing. It was warm and sweet-fragranced, that long porch in the darkness. In her childhood, she had sat in it while the thunder shuddered around her, feeling the misty whip of rain in her face while she closed her eyes and heard the soothing squeak of the swing in motion.

The sudden blinding glare of the porch

light brought a surprised gasp from her lips; she sat stark upright as Clint came into view.

It was always a shock to see him in a beige linen suit and coral silk tie, the white of his shirt bringing out his swarthy complexion, his dark hair. He could have passed for a very masculine model, sophistication clinging to his tall, muscular body like the spicy cologne he favored.

His eyes were a dark green as they swept over her blue-jeaned figure, rigid in the porch swing. He eyed her through a small gray cloud of cigarette smoke, moving closer like some big, graceful cat.

"Hiding, Irish?" he asked quietly.

She dragged her eyes down to his broad chest. "I felt like some air."

One dark eyebrow went up. "You fell out of that swing on your head once," he recalled. "You and Janna were using it for a rocking horse, and you went head over heels."

Her fingers touched the dark green

wooden frame and the cold metal chain gently. "You like to remind me of the unpleasant things, don't you?" she asked carelessly.

"Would you rather be reminded of that day by the corral when you did everything but go down on your knees and beg me to make love to you?" he asked mockingly, a harsh note in his voice that cut as much as the humiliating words.

Her eyes closed at that memory, at the pain of it. There was a streak of cruelty in him, she thought miserably; there had to be or he wouldn't enjoy taunting her like this. She got out of the swing, still avoiding his eyes, and started past him.

One lean, steely hand shot out like a bullet and caught her arm roughly, hauling her up against him as easily as if she'd been a child.

"No comeback, Irish?" he growled. "Where's that hot temper now?"

She couldn't find it. Her body trembled

in his grasp, and she couldn't even fight him.

With a gesture that was barely short of violence, he threw his unfinished cigarette off the porch and caught her by both shoulders, his fingers hurting, his green eyes blazing down into hers.

"Let me go!" she burst out, panic sweeping through her because of the new sensations he was causing her to feel as he bruised her body against him.

"Why?" he asked shortly.

Her full mouth trembled as she searched for the words that would free her. "You're...hurting me," she managed.

"Where?" he murmured, and his eyes began to sketch her small, flushed face like an artist's brush.

"My...my shoulders," she stammered.

His crushing hold loosened, became warm and sensuously caressing, his fingers burning her through the thin cotton blouse. "Does this hurt?" he asked gently.

She couldn't get the words out. He was

burning her alive with that slow, tenderly soothing touch, making her heart dance, making her lungs feel collapsed. Her small hands went to the silky shirt, pushing half-heartedly against the warm, unyielding muscles of his broad chest.

Soft, deep laughter brushed her ears. "Can't you talk to me, little Maggie?" he whispered deeply. His hands left her shoulders to cup her face and hold it up to his eyes. The warm strength in them drained her of protest, the tang of his cologne was permeating her senses. Her fingers, where they pressed against him, were so cold they felt numb. And still she couldn't move, couldn't look away from the mocking gaze that had her hypnotized, trapped.

His eyes dropped to her soft young mouth, and one thumb came up to brush across it like a whisper. "I could break your mouth open under mine like a ripe melon right now," he murmured sensuously, "and you wouldn't lift a finger to stop me, would you, Irish? You're still mine to take, any damned time I want you!''

With a sob of exquisite shame, she broke free of him, catching him off guard, and she ran every step of the way back into the house, ignoring Emma's stunned queries as she took the steps two at a time.

All the long night she lay awake, staring at the dark ceiling, planning a way, any way, out of this nightmare. Even going back to her old job, seeing Philip again, didn't hold the terror that staying here did. She had to get away. She had to!

She climbed out of bed and into her clothes numbly as the sun began to climb out of the early morning clouds. She packed before she went downstairs, her mind made up, her eyes red and dark-shadowed from lack of sleep. She'd have breakfast and explain to Emma, then she'd get a cab to the bus station, and Clint would never...

He was still at the breakfast table, where

he normally wouldn't have been at this hour of the morning. His own eyes looked as if he hadn't slept, and she wondered bitterly what time he'd come home, reasoning she must have dozed off eventually because she never heard him come in.

"I'll get you some coffee, honey," Emma said quietly, patting her on the shoulder as she passed toward the kitchen.

She made a big production of unfolding her linen napkin and smoothing it on her lap, of studying the tablecloth, of doing everything but meeting the watchful gaze across from her.

"Did you sleep at all?" he asked finally, his voice deep and slow and bitter.

"Oh, I...I slept fine, thanks," she managed.

"Like hell," he scoffed.

"Shouldn't you be out with the cattle?" she asked.

"Not until you convince me that you're not going to be on the first northbound bus," he said flatly.

That brought her eyes jerking up to meet the question in his, and he had all the answer he needed.

"I thought so," he said, leaning back in his chair to study her through narrowed eyes. "Running never solved anything, Maggie."

She glared at him, feeling something break inside her. "I need your advice like a hole in the head," she snapped, her face wounded. "What are you trying to do to me, Clint? Wasn't what Philip did to me enough without you trying to shatter the few pieces of me he left intact? Why do you enjoy hurting me?"

"Don't you know, honey?" he asked in a dangerously quiet tone.

It was the stranger's face again, not Clint's, and she stared at him curiously. "I...I don't think I know you at all sometimes," she said involuntarily.

"You don't." He gulped down the remainder of his coffee and lit a cigarette. "You're wallowing in self-pity, Irish, or didn't you realize it? Poor little girl, betrayed by her fiancé, left alone at the altar...well, I'm fresh out of sympathy. He was a damned two-timing cheat, and you're well rid of him. All he hurt was your pride, little icicle," he said ruthlessly. "You wouldn't recognize love if it came up and sat on your foot."

"I suppose you would, being such an expert!" she flashed.

His eyes glinted at her over a mocking smile. "That's more like it," he chuckled.

She frowned. "What?"

He rose, pausing by her chair on his way out, one long arm sliding in front of her as he leaned down. "I told you before, baby," he murmured at her ear, "I like it when you fight me. That's the easiest way to tell that you aren't trying to bury your head in the past."

She flushed, suddenly understanding—or, almost understanding—his behavior last night.

"I don't want to spend the whole two weeks fighting you," she grumbled.

His fingers caught her chin and raised her eyes to his. All the levity was gone from his hard, dark face now. "Why don't you get Emma to pack us a picnic lunch?" he asked softly, "and bring it down to the feedlot around noon. We'll go down by the river and eat."

"B...but, the sale; all those invitations, and the...the publicity...?" she stammered.

One long finger traced the soft curve of her mouth in a silence that made her unsteady breathing audible. "I'll lay you down under that gnarled old oak," he whispered deeply, holding her eyes, "and teach you all the things Philip should have had the patience to teach you."

She blushed furiously and tore her eyes away. "I...I really don't need any lessons, thank you," she said shortly. She jerked away from his lean hand. "Once burned, twice shy, Clint. You won't bring me to my knees again, not ever!''

He didn't seem to be fazed by her passionate outburst. He only smiled. ''Won't I? Don't underestimate me, honey.''

''I learned early not to underestimate the enemy,'' she replied.

He went out laughing just as Emma returned with the coffee and a plate of eggs, bacon, and fresh biscuits. ''Now, what's got into him?'' she asked curiously.

''The devil,'' Maggie said tightly.

Maggie was just finishing an advertisement on the sale for the local weekly paper when she heard a sudden loud pounding at the front door, and Emma's quick footsteps going to answer it. There was the snap as the door opened, and a sudden jubilant cry from Emma, and then two voices mingling, Emma's excited one and a laughing, pleasant male one.

''Maggie! Come here!'' Emma called.

Puzzled at the commotion, Maggie

stuck her head around the door and found her eyes held by a pair of dark blue ones in a deeply tanned face outlined by thick blond hair.

"Well, hush my mouth, if it isn't the girl I swore undying love to on the stage in our sixth-grade play!" Brent Halmon grinned, his eyes sparkling at her from the hall.

"Hi, Sir Got-A-Lott, where's your hawse?!" she laughed back.

He threw open the door and swung her up in his lean arms, planting a smacking kiss on her cheek. "By gosh, you've grown, Maggie!" he teased, giving her a lengthy appraisal as he set her back on her feet. "Did you really get this pretty in just four years?"

"This isn't my real face, you know," she whispered *sotto voce*. "It's the mask I wear so my green warts won't show!"

"Still got 'em, huh?" he said in mock resignation, shaking his head. "I warned you about kissing those frogs, didn't I?"

"You two!" Emma laughed, eyeing them. "Always into mischief of some sort or other. You gave Clint gray hairs when you were kids."

"Speaking of old Heavy Hand, where is he?" Brent grinned.

"Out putting diapers on his baby cows," Maggie told him. "And ribbons on their mamas, and evening jackets on their daddies. There's a sale day coming up next week."

"I know," Brent told her, "that's why I came. I've got my eye on that prize Hereford bull of Cousin Clint's."

"Speaking of mammoth ranches," Maggie said, "how is Mississippi?"

"Green and beautiful. Why don't you ever come to visit me?"

She shrugged. "Work. As a matter of fact, I'm Clint's temporary secretary for the next couple of weeks. That's why I'm here."

He nodded. "I heard about Lida taking a powder on him," Brent said with a harsh sigh. "It was no less than I expected. I thought Clint of all people would have more sense…"

"And I think everyone's got the wrong idea," Emma said quietly. "Clint wasn't in love with Lida. He wasn't thinking of marriage, either. He's a normal, healthy man, and she was a sophisticated woman who knew the score. And that's enough about it. Come on, Brent, I'll show you up. Clint will be so surprised…!"

"See you in a few minutes, Mag," Brent called over Emma's bright conversation.

Brent was changing for supper when Clint came in, dusty and tired and in a gruff temper. His eyes narrowed as they settled on Maggie, finishing one last letter at her desk.

"Weren't you hungry?" he asked without preamble.

She stared at him blankly. "Hungry?"

"At dinner," he said flatly.

She remembered what he'd told her at

breakfast and began to bloom with color. "You were joking..." she said weakly.

"The hell I was," he shot back, his eyes narrow, threatening.

She opened her mouth to speak just as Brent came in the door and clapped Clint on the back.

"Hi, Cousin!" he said cheerfully as Clint wheeled, stunned, to face him. "Surprise, surprise!"

"My God, what are you doing here?" Clint asked irritably.

"I came for the sale," was the imperturbable reply. "You did invite me," he reminded the older man.

"For the sale, not the summer!"

Brent's eyebrows went up, but he cheerfully ignored Clint's ill humor. "Bull gore you or something?" he asked pleasantly, studying the taller man's dusty clothes for sign of blood.

Maggie stifled a giggle, but not before Clint shot a narrow glance her way and saw her face.

"Oh, you're home!" Emma smiled at Clint from the doorway. "Just look who's here. Isn't it nice to have Brent back again?"

"Enchanting," Clint agreed. "Pardon me while I go upstairs and put a gun to my temple in honor of the occasion."

Three pairs of puzzled eyes followed his tall figure as he thudded up the stairs.

"He doesn't *look* drunk," Brent remarked casually.

Clint's temper seemed to have improved when he came back downstairs, his dark hair still damp from a shower, in a pair of dark slacks and a green patterned silk shirt open at the neck, in a shade that matched his eyes. He seemed to go out of his way to be pleasant to Brent, dwelling on the subject of cattle and land management to such an extent that Emma and Maggie ignored them and talked clothes all through the meal.

"I haven't been around back yet," Brent said as they relaxed over coffee in the living room. "Is the pool still there, and filled?"

"It is," Clint said pleasantly. "Feel like a swim? Maggie?" he added, glancing at her.

"If you'll let me wear a bathing suit, instead of pushing me in fully clothed," she said sweetly.

"Honey, it'll be a pleasure," he said in a voice that made chills run down her spine.

"Did I miss something?" Brent blinked.

"Last summer," Maggie explained, "he threw me in the river with my clothes on."

"You kicked the hell out of me first," Clint replied imperturbably.

"What was I supposed to do, stand there and let the stupid snake have first bite?!"

"Did you think you could stone the damned thing to death with a handful of pebbles?"

"They were stones, and I...!"

Brent stood up. "If you two want to do this thing properly, why don't you appoint seconds and meet in the lower pasture at sunup?"

Clint gave him a look that sent him toward the stairs. "I'm going after my trunks. Coming, Maggie?"

She glared at Clint. "Why not?"

Four

The pool was Olympic-sized, and the water was pleasantly cool. Maggie floated quietly, her slender body scantily covered in an aqua two-piece bathing suit, her long hair floating behind her. She and Brent had done two laps paralleling each other when Clint joined them. Swimming was something he rarely did in company, and never among strangers. A long, jagged white scar ran from the center of his broad, hair-laden chest along the bronzed skin of his flat stomach. Another was visible on his muscular thigh. Souvenirs, he called them, of a long-ago conflict when he hadn't quite dived away in time to miss a shower of shrapnel. To Maggie, they weren't in the least unsightly—the only thing about him that shook her was the sight of that powerful, dark body without the veneer of clothing to make it less sensuous. But Clint was touchy about his scars nevertheless, so she never mentioned them, nor did Brent.

They relaxed in the soothing water without talking for lazy minutes, until Emma shattered the peace by calling Brent to the phone.

"They find you wherever you go," Brent groaned as he pulled his slender body out of the water. "Carry on without me, Maggie. Clint'll save you if you go down for the third time."

"Want to bet?" she murmured, but he hadn't heard her.

Clint surfaced beside her, shaking his dark head to throw his hair out of his eyes, and his lean hands caught her bare midriff, sending a wild shudder of pleasure through her slim body as he righted her in the water and pulled her body against him roughly.

"What was that crack supposed to mean?" he asked, his eyes burning into hers, his muscular legs entwining with hers under the water.

"That you'd probably enjoy drowning me," she said unsteadily. Chills began to run over her. "Please let me go. I'm cold."

"Cold or excited?" he asked, his face solemn, his gaze level and questioning. "You always had a soft spot for Brent, didn't you, Irish?"

"We get along very well."

"And you and I don't," he said flatly.

"That goes without saying. Clint..." Her hands pushed against him, touching the thick scar at his breastbone. Her eyes drifted down to it lying under the thick tangle of wet hair that felt strange and new to her touch. Her fingers traced it gently, then they moved over the broad, hard chest that was cool from the water. A shock went through her as she realized what she was doing and she jerked her hand away as though his flesh had scorched her.

He caught her hand and lifted it to his shoulder, holding it there as he studied her downcast face. "Maggie, don't," he said gently.

"I'm sorry," she murmured in a whipped tone. "I didn't mean to..."

He caught a handful of her wet hair and pushed her face against him until it was smothered against the cool, bronzed flesh, the curling hairs tickling her nose.

"My God, I like it when you touch me," he whispered at her ear, a husky, strange note in his voice. "There's nothing to be ashamed of. It's natural for a woman to be curious, especially when she's innocent." His fingers tightened at her nape.

Against her, under the water, she could feel the heavy, hard beat of his heart. "Come here, honey," he whispered, and both arms went around her, swallowing her, in an embrace that brought the stars down into the pool with them. His hold tightened slowly, holding her, crushing her, hurting her...

"Give me your mouth," he growled huskily.

Burning, hungry, she lifted her face to his blazing eyes and saw them shift to her lips with something like awe. This was Clint—Clint, who teased her and tormented her, who was as much a part of her childhood as the ranch, the horses, Janna. But it had never been like this, not in all her wild young imaginings. He was a man, older than she, experienced, confident. And her inexperience was no match for the hunger she read in his face.

"And now," he whispered roughly, bending his dark head, "now I'm going to teach you sensations you never knew you could feel, little innocent. I'm going to show you how to be a woman..."

She was trembling, helpless as she waited breathlessly to feel his hard, chiseled mouth on hers. She started to speak, to say something, anything, just as the patio door opened and broke the spell.

She felt the shudder run through Clint's hard body as he released her and dove under the water. Brent came running, his bare feet thudding on the wet concrete, and dove into the water with a resounding splash.

Maggie went riding with Brent the next day when she finished Clint's terse correspondence, which he left for her on the Dictaphone.

"I love this place," Brent said with a smile, drinking in the lush green forest around them. "I spent a lot of my childhood here."

She smiled, too. "So did I. Janna and I used to play cowboys and Indians here, remember? Once we ambushed you from the top of one of those pines.''

''And got ticks, both of you,'' he remembered gleefully.

She shuddered. ''It was awful!''

''No doubt.'' He stopped and looked down at her, frowning. ''What got into Clint last night?'' he asked suddenly.

She felt the blush rising, and averted her face. ''Bad temper,'' she said flatly, remembering how he'd left the pool without a backward glance just after Brent's return. He had left the house not long afterward, and it had been early morning before Maggie heard the car return. By the time she and Brent got to the breakfast table, he was already at work. She closed her eyes on the memory of what he'd been about to do—what she'd almost let him do. She could still see his hard mouth poised just above hers, feel his warm, smoky breath mingling with her own. She'd wanted that kiss so much that it was like being torn apart when Brent had interrupted them.

But it was better this way, she reminded herself. Clint had all the women he needed, that was obvious. He liked to humiliate her, anyway, so she should have been better armored. Perhaps now that Brent was here...

"Where are you?" Brent asked, waving a hand in front of her eyes.

She glanced at him with wide eyes. "Mars," she whispered theatrically, "out there! Exploring strange and exotic places with my mind!"

He grinned. "Why not try exploring me with your lips?" he leered, raising and lowering his eyebrows for effect.

She burst out laughing and let Melody flow into step beside his horse. "You're just what I needed. Oh, I'm so glad you came!"

"I'm glad *you* are," he replied.

"What do you mean?"

He glanced at her speculatively. "I mean, Cousin Clint isn't. Look out, my long-ago leading lady. Clint in action is a force to behold.''

''I don't understand.''

''He wants you,'' he told her nonchalantly.

Her heart stopped, then started again. ''He's only playing games, Brent. Lida ripped at his pride and...''

''He wants you,'' he repeated quietly. ''I've never seen him look at a woman exactly that way before, but the intent is all too familiar. I wouldn't like to see you hurt.''

His concern was comforting. She reached out and touched his thin arm. ''I don't want to see me hurt, either,'' she said with a smile. ''I've got both eyes wide open. I'm not burying my head in the sand.''

He shook his head, smiling back. ''My sweet, you've been in love with him most of your life, pseudo-fiancés notwithstanding. He may not see it, but I do.''

She chewed on her bottom lip, staring

down at the pommel of her saddle. "I thought Philip would…"

"…Compensate?" he finished for her. "You knew better, didn't you? Maggie, you shouldn't have come here."

She laughed softly. "It's a little late now."

"Come home with me when I leave," he said quietly.

She stared at him, trying to read his thin face.

"No, it isn't like that," he laughed. "Maggie," he added, solemn now, "I know how you feel. There's a woman back home…I'd give everything I own, and more; she doesn't feel that way about me. And, like you, I know that nobody else could take her place. Don't let yourself be drawn and quartered like this. We'll console each other."

"A shoulder to cry on, Brent?" she asked softly.

"That's all I can offer you," he replied, more serious than she'd ever seen him. He grinned suddenly. "Did you think I was offering you a grand passion?"

She laughed feverishly. "Let me think about it. Right now, I'm doing a job, and I gave my word."

"It's up to you what you do," he replied. "I never try to actively interfere in anyone else's life. But I'm offering you a refuge if ever you need it. And he'll never find you."

She nodded. "Thanks for the option."

He winked at her. "You're more my cousin than he is. We always were a pair of rascals."

"We still are." She leaned toward him conspiratorially. "Let's swipe the rotor out of his jeep."

"You're on!"

Clint eyed both of his innocent-looking guests over the supper table.

"A strange thing happened to me today," he remarked casually. "I tried to start my jeep and the rotor was missing."

"The rotor?" Emma exclaimed, pausing in the act of lifting a forkful of mashed potatoes to her mouth. "The rotor was gone?"

Maggie raised both eyebrows and met Clint's searching gaze levelly. "How strange," she said impassively.

Brent strangled on his coffee and had to excuse himself from the table.

"Never fear!" Maggie called after him, rising. "First aid is on the way!"

For the next few days, she and Brent fortunately were able to keep out of Clint's way—just. But his temper was shorter than ever, and getting things ready for the mammoth sale wasn't helping it.

"Hey, Maggie," Billy Jones, the foreman called, "Clint wants to see you!"

She looked up from the porch where she was getting a checklist ready for the midday barbecue at the sale. "Well, here I am!" she called cheerfully. "Tell him to look to his heart's content!"

Billy went away shaking his head, and

Maggie was instantly sorry. Brent had just been called away on business that morning and she was afraid to push Clint too far without Brent's protection. But the tension was beginning to get to her...

"So there you are, you damned little witch," Clint muttered, coming up the steps, his hat cocked over his brow, fury in every line of his hard face.

She felt herself cringing, but she kept her eyes raised. "Yes?"

He stopped just in front of her and swept off his hat, slinging it onto the nearby table. He leaned down, one hard-muscled arm on either side of her where she sat in the big, high-backed rocking chair, trapping her.

"If I were you," he said in a dangerously soft voice, "I wouldn't push too hard. I've had about all I can take from you and Cousin Brent!"

She felt the raw power in that lean body at the proximity, and it was disturbing. "Just because we hid your rotor..."

"...*And* tied pink ribbons on the tails of two of my milk cows, *and* put bubble bath in the swimming pool, and..." he growled hotly.

She flushed. It had really been funny at the time. "Your trouble is that you don't have a sense of humor," she grumbled.

"You've got enough for both of us!" he shot back. His eyes were like a panther's—green-gold in that swarthy face, narrow and threatening.

"Even when Brent and I were kids, you managed to make us feel like criminals every time we played a prank," she told the open front of his blue-checked shirt, where dark, curling hair peeked out, damp with sweat.

"You damned near turned my hair white a few times," he recalled, and some of the anger drained out of him. He smiled.

"So I see," she murmured, and involuntarily her fingers reached up to touch the silver at his temples. "You're absolutely *sure* it isn't a sign of old age?'' she added mischievously.

He chuckled softly. ''You brat.''

All the years seemed to fall away when he laughed like that, and he was the Clint of her childhood, the bigger-than-life creature her dreams were made of, invulnerable and indestructible.

''Clint, I am sorry about the bubble bath,'' she said, ''but it did look so pretty...''

He tweaked a long strand of her hair. ''Brent's a bad influence on you. And from now on keep your little hands off my jeep.''

''Yes, Clint.''

''So meek!'' he drawled. His eyes dropped to her mouth and lingered there for a long time. Abruptly he caught her tiny waist with both hands and jerked her up against him, holding her so tightly that she cried out involuntarily.

''You beast, will you let me go?'' she gasped angrily.

His breath was warm at her temple. "It's dangerous to stop fighting me, Irish," he murmured in a stranger's husky voice. "I'm a man, not a boy like Brent, and I'm not used to limits of any kind. Are you too innocent to understand that, or do you want me to spell it out?"

She felt the lean, hard body against hers go taut as his hands put her away, and she moved to pick up the sheets of paper and pen that had fallen to the floor.

"I seem to remember your telling me that I didn't...appeal to you *that* way," she said through tight lips, avoiding his watchful gaze.

There was a long, static silence between them. "Do you have a list for Shorty?" he asked after a while, and she heard the click of his lighter just before a cloud of smoke drifted around her. "He'll need to get those supplies today so that he can start cooking early in the morning."

"I've just about finished it," she replied, sitting back down. "I thought I'd have him get some paper tablecloths and plates and napkins, too, and plastic utensils.''

"Thrifty little soul, aren't you?'' he asked gruffly. "Am I supposed to be impressed?''

"The only thing that might impress you,'' she returned hotly, "is a steam roller!''

"More depressing than impressing, surely,'' he said with a flash of a grin.

She drew a hard sigh. "You are without doubt, the most maddening human being…!''

"With your hair loose like that,'' he murmured, "and your eyes like green buds in early spring, you're pretty maddening yourself, honey. Just make sure you don't fling any of that sweet magic in Brent's direction. I'd hate like hell to have to throw him off the property.''

"What I do with Brent…!'' she began.

"…Is *my* business as long as you're on *my* ranch,'' he said flatly, his eyes daring her to argue about it. "Don't make the mistake of underestimating him, either. He's a man, and the kind of teasing you do with him can be just as inviting as a come-on."

Her mouth flew open. "Clint, for heaven's sake, I've played at words with him all my life!"

"And while you were still eight, and he was ten, it was safe." His dark green eyes swept over her lithe figure in the soft tan blouse and slacks. "Baby, you're a hell of a long way past your eighth birthday. Don't tempt fate."

"How strange that you should be warning me about Brent," she flung at him, "when just the other day he was warning me about you!"

One eyebrow went up and she could see the mischief sparkling in his eyes. "What did he say?" he asked.

Her mouth opened to say the words just as she realized what they were and shut it again. Her face burned like fire.

He laughed softly. "Well?" he prodded. "You know I'm not going to let that drop until you tell me. What did he say, Maggie?"

She shifted uneasily. "He said you were a force to behold," she said finally.

"And what else?"

"That was...all," she faltered.

He studied her for a long time, idly drawing on the cigarette. "I think I can guess," he mused. "And he's right, up to a point. I can have damned near any woman I want. But, Maggie," he added, his voice soft now, "I don't rob cradles."

She kept her eyes down, inclined to argue, but too smart to open that can of worms. "How soon do you need this list?"

"In an hour. I've got to send Shorty into town anyway for some wire I ordered. Since mother's not going to be back for two or three more months," he added, "you'll have to act as hostess."

"Can't Emma...?"

"Honey, there's nothing like a pretty, sexy woman to keep buyers happy," he taunted.

The open glare she shot up at him was as potent as words. "I will not be used as a...!"

He leaned down, his warm breath mingling with hers, stopping the tirade effectively just by moving close. His eyes burned deep into hers. "Twelve years," he murmured, "and you still can't tell when I'm teasing and when I'm not. I don't intend using you as bait. And if any man lays a finger on you, I'll break both his arms. Satisfied?"

Her eyes widened, her whole expression puzzled. "Clint, why do you...?"

His finger tapped her nose lightly. "Finish your list. I'm up to my neck in work."

He turned abruptly and left her staring after him.

Sale day came all too soon the next morning as the buyers started arriving by

car and plane. In no time at all, the lush
grounds were covered with them. Shorty
was trying to be ten places at once, busy
with roasting huge carcasses for barbecue,
stirring baked beans, making rolls—Maggie volunteered to help, but he wouldn't
hear of it, gesturing angrily at her flowing
white dress and demanding to know how
she'd ever get grease spots out. She left
him to do it with a smile and a wink. Seconds later, Emma barged in with her apron
already spotted and stained, and started
watching the beans. Shorty almost fell on
her shoulder and kissed her.

Maggie supervised the temporary help,
getting tables set up, coffee urns arranged,
tea made and tubs brought in for soft
drinks and beer. She remembered sale days
in her childhood, when Mrs. Raygen had
made this seem so easy. It was anything
but.

Unconsciously, she searched the nearby
stalls for Clint and found him with her
eyes. A tall, slender, beautiful blond

woman held onto him while he talked cattle with an elderly man beside her. There was something so familiar about the woman; she searched her memory and came up with a name. Sarah Mede. Little Sarah, who'd grown into a siren, and was chasing Clint as wholeheartedly as Maggie ever had at the precocious age of nine. Maggie sighed wearily. Janna had said something about Sarah and her father being on vacation in Europe. Apparently they were back, and she didn't need to ask who Clint had been dating recently. That possessive little jeweled hand said it all.

She turned back to her chores, wishing with all her heart that Brent could have made it back in time to give her some moral support. She felt as if she'd never needed it more. If only she'd never come!

"Well, hello," came a smooth masculine voice from behind and she turned to find a fortyish, rather attractive man in a rust-colored leisure suit standing behind her.

She smiled automatically. "Hello. Here for the sale?" she asked.

He smiled down at her. "That's why I came," he drawled with a laugh in his voice. "But I hear Clint's cousin already put in a bid for Bighorn. I sure had my heart set on that old Hereford bull."

"Sorry," she said with a smile. "But Brent did, too."

"You one of the family?"

She shook her head. "I'm Clint's temporary secretary. But I grew up just a few minutes north of here. I've known Clint and Janna and Brent most of my life."

"I hate to be pushy, but do you think I could get a cup of coffee while we wait on that barbecue?" he asked. "I flew out of Austin without breakfast, or coffee, or a kind word from my housekeeper, and I'm just about dry."

"There's beer if you'd rather," she said, thinking he looked more like a beer man than a coffee one.

He grinned, making extra lines in his

swarthy face. "Can't stomach the stuff," he said with quiet honesty. "Although I will admit to a taste for aged Scotch. But right now all I want is coffee."

"Then, that's what you'll get, Mister...?"

"Masterson," he replied. "Duke Masterson. You?"

"Maggie Kirk."

"Just Maggie?" he probed.

She shrugged. "Well, actually, it's Margaretta Leigh," she told him, "but nobody ever calls me that."

"Why not?" he asked gently. "I think it's lovely."

She felt very young under those quiet, dark eyes, and out of her depth. "Let's see about that coffee."

He was a cattleman, as she guessed, with a large ranch near Austin as well as real estate and oil holdings. He was also an attractive man, with a charm that put her immediately at ease.

"I've been overseas for a month or so,"

he told her over a cup of steaming black coffee. "In Greece."

The question was out before she realized it. "Did you go to see Pompeii?"

It seemed to startle him. "Why, yes, I did. And Troy, and the Acropolis." He leaned forward. "Don't tell me you're an archaeology nut."

"I spent my childhood climbing over Indian mounds, and I read everything I can lay my hands on about new digs," she admitted.

"By God," he whispered. "Sounds like me. I used to follow my father down the rows as he plowed and pick up arrowheads, and pieces of pottery. I spend as much time as I can..."

"Tired, Masterson?" came a quiet, deep voice from just behind Maggie.

Masterson chuckled. "Beat, Clint," he admitted. "I got two hours of sleep last night and flew out without breakfast or even a cup of instant coffee. Margaretta took pity on me."

Clint moved into view with Sarah Mede still attached to his arm. He looked down at Maggie with strange, probing eyes. "Margaretta?" he murmured curiously.

Maggie bristled. "It is my name."

"And a very pretty one," Masterson added, sipping his coffee. "Clint, how about letting me borrow her for the evening? Just long enough for company at the supper table, at least."

The question seemed to surprise Clint as much as it did Maggie.

"I'd love to!" Maggie said without thinking. "We can talk some more about archaeology!"

"Archaeology?" Clint burst out, his eyes narrow and darkening. "What the hell do you know about that?"

She glared at him. "Quite a lot, in fact. I had two courses in it at University, and I spent two months on a dig just last year!"

"I don't see what you're so upset about, Clint, honey," Sarah murmured softly, and smiled at Maggie. "It isn't often that two people find something like that in common. And so quickly, too. Well, as you and I both like country-western music, Clint," she explained.

"I'll take care of her," Masterson told Clint, and something in his eyes seemed to convince the younger man. "I think you know me well enough, don't you?"

"I do," Clint said finally, his voice deep and quiet. "And you can take that as a compliment. There aren't many men I could say that about."

"What is this?" Maggie grumbled, glaring at Clint. "I'm a grown woman. I don't need a watchdog!"

"Grown," Clint scoffed. "Twenty, and you've got all the answers, is that it?"

"But, Clint," Sarah cooed, "I'm just twenty-one, and you never fuss about me..."

"Shut up, Sarah," he said flatly.

"You'd never say that to me," Maggie told him. "I'd flatten you like a...!"

"Go to hell, Maggie," Clint said with a hellish smile, and turning, drew Sarah along with him. "Get her home by midnight, Masterson," he called over his shoulder. "She turns into a pumpkin if you don't."

Masterson smiled at her. "Do you?" he asked, watching the emotions working on her wan face.

"I wish he would," she whispered hotly. "I don't need a big brother any more."

"I think you do." He folded his arms on the table and studied her. "I'm forty-two years old, little girl. And I'll guarantee that if Clint didn't know me personally, you'd never set foot outside this yard with me. But I don't have designs on you, and he knows that, too. I just need company, and it's very pleasant to have a conversation with someone who understands carbon dating and the lure of ancient tombs."

She smiled. "Thank you."

Both his heavy eyebrows went up.

"Thank *you*. Now, how would you like to hear about Pompeii?"

"Oh, I'd love it!" she replied, and settled down to listen, trying not to hear Clint's last angry words, trying to forget the hatred in his eyes...

The sale was over, the guests leaving, bare bones where the barbecued steer carcasses had been, when Maggie left with Masterson for the restaurant.

Clint had gone off with Sarah, and it was a blessed relief. She'd had about all the battle she could stomach for one day.

Over a nicely grilled steak, Masterson shared some of his journeys with her, smiling at the rapt expression on her young face as he described places she'd have given worlds to see.

"I've always wanted to see Stonehenge," she told him.

"Then why not go?" he asked. "Air fares aren't all that high, you know."

She smiled. "And I could always volunteer for a dig. It's just time. There never seems to be enough.''

Something darkened his eyes for an instant. "I know. Don't let yours run out before you do a few of the things you want to do, little girl.''

She shrugged. "I've got plenty.''

"No," he said softly, his eyes distant. "No, none of us has plenty.''

It was midnight on the nose when Masterson pulled his rented car up in front of the ranch house.

"I enjoyed that so much," Maggie told him with a smile. "If you ever get to Columbus…''

"That's not on the books, little one," he said gently. His dark eyes smiled at her. "Thank you for keeping an old man company. Someday you'll understand how much it meant.''

"Old man? You?" she asked incredulously.

He chuckled. "Now, that was a compliment. Goodnight, Margaretta Leigh.''

"No goodnight kiss?" she asked saucily. "I think I'm insulted."

"You little minx..." He pulled her against his big, husky body and kissed her, hard and slow and with an expertise that was shattering. "Thank you, Maggie," he whispered, as he let her go.

"Goodnight," she told him, sliding reluctantly out of the car.

"Goodbye, honey," he replied softly. And in seconds, he was gone.

She stood watching the car's taillights as it wound around the driveway toward the highway, and for just an instant she wasn't in Florida at all. She was standing on the ruins of an ancient civilization with the breeze stirring her hair and drums pounding in her blood. And he was there, too, but his name wasn't Masterson. She shivered. Another time, another place, those dark eyes had looked into hers and today in a few hours out of time his soul had reached out to touch hers. She felt ripples of emotion tingling through her taut body. How strange to meet and instinctively know all about him—as if in another life...

"Come inside, little one."

She turned to meet Clint. He was still wearing his suit pants and his white shirt, but his tie and his jacket were gone. He looked dangerously attractive.

"I...I was just watching the car," she murmured as they went up the steps. The shiver went through her again and without thinking she slid her cold hand into Clint's, like a child seeking comfort. For just an instant his hand tensed. Then it curled, lean and hard, around hers and squeezed it.

"What's wrong, honey?" he asked.

She shook her head. "I felt...as if I'd known him somewhere before. And something was wrong, I felt it!"

"Déjà vu?" he asked with a smile, leading her into the house, and then into his den.

She shrugged, dropping wearily down

onto the sofa. "I guess. I don't know. It frightened me." She watched him pour a neat whiskey, drop ice into it, and toss it back. "Tell me about him."

Clint moved across the room and went down on one knee beside her, his darkening eyes almost on a level with her in the position. His hands caught hers where they lay in her lap.

"He's got cancer, honey," he said very gently. "There's nothing they can do for him, and from what he told me himself, he's got less than two more months."

A sob broke from her and tears rolled down her cheeks. "I like him," she murmured through a pale smile.

"So do I. A hell of a man, Masterson. I've known him most of my life." He took his handkerchief and mopped her eyes. "You know, he accomplished more in his forty-two years than most men do in a lifetime. He didn't waste a second of it. It's hard to grieve too much for a man like that."

She looked into his quiet eyes for a long time. "I...I can't picture you grieving for anyone," she said softly.

"Can't you, honey?" He smiled at her, gently, his hand smoothing the hair away from her damp cheeks. "Do you still think I'm invulnerable?"

"I don't know." She studied his dark, quiet face for a long time. "I don't know very much about you at all. I...I didn't even know you liked country-western music."

"I like any kind of music. And storms, the wilder the better. And sensitive young women with liquid jade for eyes," he whispered deeply. "And if you weren't still cherishing that kiss Masterson gave you out in the car, I'd take your mouth and make you beg for mine, little girl."

She blushed to the roots of her hair, and tried to steady her breathing so that he wouldn't notice the effect those soft words had on her fragile emotions.

"I...I might not even...even like it,"

she replied, struggling for even a small surge of indignation to use against him.

"You've spent the past four years wondering how my mouth would feel on yours," he said quietly, his eyes biting into hers. "We both know that."

Shakily, she got to her feet and moved around him toward the door.

"When are you going to stop running from me?" he asked, as her hand went to the doorknob.

"Goodnight, Clint," she replied, ignoring the question.

"Don't trip on your way to the nursery," he growled.

She could taste the bitterness in those harsh words, and it served him right to be thwarted. For pure conceit, he was unbeatable.

"Margaretta."

The breathless sound of her name on his lips, so strange, so unfamiliar, made her freeze. She turned to catch an expression on his face that she couldn't understand.

"Go riding with me tomorrow," he said gently. "I'll take you down to that little branch of the creek where you and Janna used to go wading."

She hesitated. "Why?" she asked.

"Maybe I want to get to know you again," he said carelessly.

"Did you ever know me?" she asked him.

He shook his head. "I'm beginning to think I didn't. Will you come?"

She chewed on her lower lip. "If...if Brent isn't home, I will."

His eyes narrowed, a muscle in his jaw working. "Brent isn't coming back," he said tautly. "He called while you were out and asked me to ship his bull to Mississippi. He's on his way to Hong Kong."

"Oh." She turned away.

"Don't look so damned lost! My God, Irish, how many men does it take for you lately?" he growled hotly.

"What does it matter to you?" she shot back.

He still hadn't answered her when she went upstairs.

Five

He was waiting for her at the breakfast table, a red knit shirt stretched across the broad expanse of his chest with bronzed flesh and curling dark hair just visible in the V-neck. His pale eyes searched hers for an instant before they dropped to the eggshell blue blouse over her blue jeans. They narrowed on the thin ribbon that bound her hair at the nape of her neck.

"Why did you drag your hair back like that?" he asked quietly.

"It gets in my eyes when I ride," she replied, taking her seat at the table.

"How do you want your eggs, sweet?" Emma called from the kitchen.

"None for me, Emma! Just coffee this morning," she called back.

"No appetite?" Clint chided.

She looked up into his eyes. "No," she said in a voice that sounded breathless even to her own ears.

Smiling, he studied her over the rim of his coffee cup. "No makeup?" he asked gently.

She watched the light catch the silver threads in his hair and make them burn. "I...I haven't put it on yet."

He held her eyes across the table, his face solemn. "Don't. I don't like the taste of it."

Her lips parted on a protest, but Emma came in with a steaming cup of coffee and Maggie gave it her wholehearted attention.

It was a perfect morning for a lazy horseback ride. Even the sweltering heat was unnoticeable under the shade of the mammoth pecan trees in the sprawling orchard. Maggie never failed to be impressed with the orderly lines they'd been planted in so many years before.

"I wonder how old they are," she murmured absently.

"The trees?" Clint smiled. "Older than either one of us, that's a fact."

"Speak for yourself, Grandpa," she returned impishly.

He slanted a vengeful glance her way and pulled his hat low over his brow. "Dangerous ground, Maggie."

"I'm not afraid of you," she teased. "Your poor old bones are so brittle they'd probably break if you chased me."

He reined in his stallion and glared at her. "I think Brent had a point," he told her. "How about guns at fifty paces tomorrow morning?"

"Are you sure your hand's steady enough to hold a gun...?"

"Damn you!" he laughed.

She laughed back, and the years nearly fell away. "Race you to the meadow!" she called, and put her heels to Melody's flanks.

She thought she had him beat as they rode across the green pasture with its scattering of wildflowers and headed toward the woods. But before she could reach them, Clint passed her as if the small mare she rode was backing up. No one, she thought miserably, could beat him at this. He was a superb horseman, almost part of the horse he rode, and a study in masculine grace and power.

"Where've you been?" he asked as she reined up beside him. He paused in the act of lighting a cigarette to grin at her flushed, angry face. "Sore loser!"

She made a face at him. "Why do you always have to win?"

"It's my land," he replied nonchalantly.

Her eyes swung over the lush, grassy pasture to the fences far away in the distance, to the herds of cattle that looked like red and white dots. "It's beautiful," she murmured softly.

"You didn't always think so," he reminded her. "And you were right. Ranch life has its drawbacks, Maggie. There isn't much night life around here, much excitement. It can get pretty lonely."

"Is that how I strike you?" she asked with a wistful smile. "A city girl with a passion for nightclubs?"

He studied her narrowly over his cigarette. "Definitely a city girl. You always were."

She let her eyes follow the flight of a vivid yellow and black butterfly nearby. "I'm glad you know me so well."

There was an explosive silence. "If you hate the city so damned much, why do you live there?"

She flinched at the quiet fury in his voice. "What else could I do? All I know how to be is a secretary." She glared at him. "There aren't many jobs available for women cowhands, in case you've forgotten. Or is it," she added coldly, "that you just never noticed I wasn't a boy?"

His eyes twinkled with humor. "To tell the truth, honey, I never gave it much thought."

She touched the mare's flanks gently and urged her into a walk. "Thanks."

The path through the woods was wide enough for both horses to walk abreast— more a fire road than a trail. The peace was hypnotic, only broken by the soft swish of the pines in the breeze, the near-far sound of bubbling, soft-running water.

"This way," Clint said, turning his mount down a smaller, less clear path.

She followed him to what seemed to be a wall of underbrush. He stepped down out of the saddle and tied the stallion, motioning Maggie to tie the mare several yards beyond.

He held the branches back for her, and as she strode forward into the small clearing, it was suddenly like stepping back through time. The tiny stream where she

and Janna once spent lazy summer after-
noons wading and sharing dreams over a
picnic lunch was there. As clear and sweet
and sandy as ever.

"Watch where you walk," he cautioned
her as he settled his tall form under a low-
hanging oak. "I've had cattle mire down
in that soft sand."

She glared at him as she sat down to
pull off her socks and boots. "If I moo
politely, will you haul me out?"

He grinned under the concealing brim of
his hat, as he lay back with his hands under his head. "I might."

She waded into the clear stream, de-
lighting at the feel of the cold water on her
bare feet, the damp smell of sand and silt
and sweet wildflowers along the banks.

"I used to come here when I was a
boy," he remarked lazily. "I learned to
swim just a few yards downstream where
it widens out."

"And catch tadpoles and spring lizards,
too, I'll bet."

"Nope. Just water moccasins," he replied.

She froze in her tracks. "In...here?" she asked.

"Sure. It used to be full of them."

Chills washed up her arms. She froze in the middle of the stream, warily looking around her. Suddenly every thin stick she saw was a hissing enemy.

"C...Clint? What do I do if I see one?" she asked.

"What did you used to do when you and Janna came here?"

"We never saw any."

"Pure luck," he remarked. He lifted the edge of his hat and peeked at her before he let it down again. "Well, Maggie, if you do see one, you'd better run like hell. It won't do a lot of good, of course, they're fast snakes and they've been known to chase people..."

She was sitting beside him with her boots and socks in hand before he finished the sentence.

He burst out laughing. "My God, I was teasing," he chuckled.

"You know how afraid I am of snakes," she muttered.

"After last summer, I've got a pretty good idea," he agreed.

She dried her feet with her socks, ignoring him.

"What did you do for amusement in Columbus?" he asked.

She wound one of the socks around her hand and stared at the diamond-sparkle on the water. She shrugged. "I spent most of my time digging up the backyard and planting things in the spring. In the summer, I liked to fish on the Chattahoochee. In the fall I'd go to the mountains with some of the other girls and watch the leaves turn. In the winter, I'd drive up to Atlanta to hear the symphony or watch the ballet." She studied the crumpled sock. "Dull things like that. I'll bet you can't stand classical music."

"In fact, I do," he said quietly. "Al-

though my tastes run to the old masters—
Dvorak, Debussy, Beethoven. I don't care
for many contemporary compositions.''

She stared at the hat over his face.
''Sarah said you liked country-western.''

''I do. And easy listening.'' His hand
fished blindly in his shirt pocket for a cigarette. ''I like art, too, little girl. I used to
drive all the way in to Tallahassee for ex-
hibits.''

''When the King Tut exhibit was in...''
she exclaimed.

''I saw it,'' he broke in. He removed the
hat and tossed it to one side, while he lit
a cigarette and looked up at her with eyes
a darker green than the leaves on the tree
overhead. ''Let your hair down. I don't
like it tied back like that.''

''You just want it to flop in my eyes so
I can't see,'' she pouted, but she loosened
the ribbon all the same, and let the black
waves fall gently to frame her face.

He reached out a long arm and his fingers caught a thick strand of it, testing the

softness. "Long and thick and silky," he murmured quietly. "Black satin."

She couldn't seem to get her breath. Her eyes drifted to the tree trunk behind him. "Do...do you still like to hunt?" she asked breathlessly.

"Only venison," he murmured. "Your eyelashes are almost too long to be real, did you know that?"

She caught a shaky breath. "Clint, hadn't we ought to..."

"Ought to what, sweetheart?" he asked softly.

She met his quiet, searching gaze and lost the rest of her breath as her eyes widened with something like shock.

Without taking his eyes from her, he flipped his cigarette into the stream and began to draw her closer to him.

"Clint...!" she whispered fearfully, pressing her small hands against his broad chest as he leaned over her, easing her back into the dry leaves and pine straw that blanketed the hard ground.

His lean fingers touched her face, gently exploring it in a silence that throbbed with controlled emotion. ''What are you afraid of?'' he asked softly.

''You,'' she whispered shakily, trembling as his fingers lightly traced her nose, her high cheekbones, her mouth.

''Why, Maggie?'' he asked, his gaze dropping intently to her mouth as his thumb rubbed across it, parting it, testing its silky softness.

Her heart raced under the soft, sweet pressure, and her eyes closed helplessly. The silence was as pure as dawn, broken only by the gentle swish of the tree limbs with their long gray beards of Spanish moss—and the erratic sound of her own breathing.

His lean fingers speared into the soft hair at her temples, holding her flushed face firmly as he bent; and she felt his firm, chiseled mouth touch her closed eyelids. His broad chest eased gently down against her in a contact that sent a shudder of pure pleasure rippling through her slenderness.

"Don't be afraid of me, little girl," he murmured against her ear. "I'm not trying to seduce you."

She blushed, swallowing nervously, and she felt his deep, soft laughter vibrate against her. Over the thin cotton shirt, her small hands pressed against the warm muscles of his chest.

His mouth, slightly parted, caressed her high cheekbone, the soft line of her jaw, her chin. "Unbutton it," he murmured absently.

"W...what?" she managed, drowning in new sensations.

"My shirt," he breathed at the corner of her mouth.

Her slender hands curled against him. "I...I can't!" she whispered shakily.

"Don't you want to touch me, little innocent?" he asked quietly. "You did that night in the pool—until you realized what you were doing."

"Clint, must you...!" she moaned.

"Hush," he whispered, his mouth moving until it was poised just above hers, so close that his warm, smoky breath mingled with hers. His hands moved on her face to tilt her chin up. "I need your mouth now, little girl, under mine, soft and warm and sweet."

Her eyelids opened briefly so that she could see him, and the look on his face made her tremble. "Clint..." she whispered tremulously.

"Tell me you want it," he whispered huskily.

A sob caught in her throat. "Oh, Clint...!"

His lips brushed against hers in a slow, unbearably tender tasting kiss that was everything she dreamed it could be. Vaguely she felt his fingers slide under her head to cup it, felt him stiffen as he began, ever so gently to deepen the kiss until it grew suddenly from a tiny spark to a bellowing flame between them.

A gasp broke from her lips at the fury of it, and her hands trembled as they went up to clutch at the broad shoulders above her. Clint. This was Clint, who taught her to ride, who bullied her, who broke her young heart that unforgettable summer—who was teaching her a lesson in ardor that nothing would ever erase from her mind or her heart. Clint, who was...loving her...!

All at once, he tore his mouth from hers and looked down at her with eyes that seemed to go up in green smoke.

One lean finger traced the soft, slightly swollen curve of her mouth in a lazy, tangible silence. "Margaretta Leigh," he whispered, his eyes sketching every line of her face. "What you know about lovemaking could be written on the head of a pin."

She jerked her eyes down to his chest. "I never pretended to be sophisticated," she said tightly. "I'm sorry if I disappointed you. May I get up now?"

"You didn't disappoint me," he said quietly, tilting her reluctant face up to his.

An irritating mist blurred him in her sight, and she hated the burr in her throat. "I don't know anything...!" she mumbled miserably.

"It makes for a hell of a change," he told her, and smiled patiently down at her. "I'm used to good-time girls who know everything, not sweet little innocents who need teaching."

Involuntarily, her fingers went up to touch the hard, firm mouth, feeling its sensuous contours. He kissed her fingers absently, his own going to the top buttons of his shirt to snap them open. He caught her searching hand and moved it down inside the opening, against the warm, slightly damp firmness of bronzed muscles and curling black hair.

With a gasp, she jerked her hand away as if it had been burned by the brief contact with his body.

His dark brows drew together, his eyes

narrowed. "My God, is even that too intimate for you?" he growled. "You damned little icicle, do you think the touch of those slender young hands, untutored as they are, could send a man into a web of uncontrollable passion?"

She flinched at the anger in his deep voice. He rolled away from her to sit up, curbed violence in the way he put a cigarette between his lips and lit it.

"Put your boots on, little miss purity," he said roughly, "and I'll see you safely home with your honor intact."

"Clint, I'm sorry, please don't...!" she began tearfully.

"You heard me." He got to his feet, making a swipe for his hat on the ground and slamming it on his head. He moved through the underbrush to the horses, leaving her to follow.

She tugged her boots on over the damp socks, fighting tears, and blindly made her way to the little mare. She swung into the saddle, refusing to even look his way. She turned her mount and kicked her velvety flanks, startling her into a gallop.

"Maggie...!" Clint called after her.

She leaned over Melody's neck, her fingers clinging to the soft mane, and urged her on recklessly. She wanted nothing more than to get away from him, and in a haze of pure panic, she forced the mare into a run.

It happened with incredible speed. One minute she was firmly in control. The next, she caught a glimpse of blue sky, a glimpse of green grass, and her body came into shuddering contact with the hard ground.

She was vaguely aware of a voice calling her, of a touch that was none too gentle. She was too winded to answer, and her head hurt. She moaned as she opened her eyes and the sky, along with Clint's dark, tight face, came into blurry focus above her.

"You damned little fool!" he thundered

at her, and the look in his eyes was frightening.

"I...fell," she managed in a winded whisper.

"And it's too damned bad you didn't break your stupid neck," he growled mercilessly. "I just may do it for you. Where do you hurt?"

Her lips trembled shakily. "My... head," she murmured.

His hands ran over her helpless body, feeling surely for breaks. His face was lined as she'd never seen it, emphasizing his age, and there was a pallor around his mouth that hinted of strain.

"M...Melody?" she got out.

"She's all right," was the terse reply. "No thanks to you," he added.

That was the proverbial straw. Tears began to flow down her cheeks in agony, her chest rising and falling jerkily with suppressed sobs.

"If you cry, so help me, I'll hit you, Maggie," he threatened darkly.

"You...big bully!" she wept. "I hate you!"

"That's no news." His arms went under her knees and her back, lifting her gently against him. "If I put you on Melody, can you hang on until we get home?"

"Yes," she replied doggedly. She'd hang on until hell froze over, just to spite him.

"We'll go slow," he said quietly, easily lifting her onto the small mare and making sure she had the reins firmly in hand. "Can you make it?"

She glared down at him with fierce green eyes. "You can bet on it," she said icily.

He ignored the anger, and the ice, and swung into the saddle himself. "Let's go."

It was the longest ride she could ever remember, and she was bathed in sweat when they reached the ranch house. Clint reached up for her just as she swayed dizzily in the saddle and carried her upstairs yelling for Emma as he went.

"What in the world...?" Emma asked in concern.

"Annie Oakley fell off," Clint said roughly. "Stay with this stupid child while I call Dr. Brown."

"I hope you trip and fall down the stairs!" Maggie called after him tearfully, wetness burning her eyes as she lay panting and disheveled, sore and miserable on the coverlet of her bed.

Emma sat down beside her and smoothed the wisps of hair out of her eyes. "Oh, my poor baby," she cooed, frowning in quiet empathy. "Does it hurt much?"

She began to cry, burying her face in Emma's apron. "I hate him," she sobbed. "Oh, I hate him, I..."

"I know," Emma said gently. "I've always known. Men can be so very blind, Maggie, and so hurtful. That one more than most. I've never known him to care about a woman. It's as if he's afraid of any

deep emotional involvement. Even Lida—
that was a physical thing, you know.''

"Everything…with him is…physical,''
she wept.

"His father loved his mother deeply,''
Emma recalled, gently smoothing the dark
waving hair on her knee. "But Mrs. Raygen was never able to return that love,
even though she was fond of him. Perhaps
the age difference was really too much.
But Clint sensed that lack of balance in his
parents' marriage, and it affected him.
Love is a word he doesn't understand, my
darling,'' she sighed. "I'm sorry it's taken
you so many years, and so much heartache, to learn it.''

"Oh, Emma, so am I,'' she whispered.

Six

Dr. Brown wanted to see her immediately, and she went reluctantly with Clint to his office to spend over an hour being X-rayed and probed and checked from head to toe. It was a mild concussion, and she was sent home with orders to stay in bed for at least twenty-four hours and for Clint to contact him if there were any nausea or unusual sleepiness.

"I'm sorry for the inconvenience,"

Maggie said tersely on the way home, drowsy already from the office visit and emotional stress. "I'll make up my work."

He took a long draw from his cigarette. "No sweat, Maggie," he said.

She leaned her head against the window, closing her eyes. She was already asleep when they got back home, not even aware of being carried upstairs and tucked in her bed. Not aware of the tall, solemn figure that sat quietly watching her for the better part of an hour with an intensity that would have shaken her if she'd seen it.

The next day, she was sore and stiff, but the headache had eased, and some of the heartache with it. Another week and she could go back to the apartment, and Janna, and a new job, and leave all this behind. All this. Clint. Clint! Her eyes closed miserably. This time, she'd have to leave him behind for good. No more trips to the ranch, ever, not even for a few days in the summer, and Emma wouldn't understand and neither would Janna. There'd have to be a very good excuse by then. Maybe if she had an overseas job...

"You'll have premature wrinkles if you keep scowling like that," Clint remarked from the doorway.

She spared him a quick glance, noting that he was dressed in a neat gray business suit instead of his jeans, and his dark head was bare. He looked more like a businessman than a rancher—and devilishly attractive.

"Going away, I hope?" she asked sweetly, concentrating on her cold hands.

"For a few days," he replied, a mocking smile touching his hard mouth. "I thought that might cheer you up."

"It's doing wonders for my disposition," she agreed.

There was a long pause before he shouldered away from the door and came to stand beside the bed, his eyes dark green and strangely solemn as he looked down at her.

"Head better?" he asked.

She nodded. "Lots, thanks."

"Look at me."

The quiet note in his deep voice brought her eyes up to meet his in a silence laced with tension.

"I want to know," he said, "why you were afraid to touch me that day by the stream."

She felt and hated the color that warmed her cheeks. "It's over, can't we just...?"

"Hell, no, we can't!" he shot back, his whole look threatening. He sat down beside her on the bed. "Tell me."

She pressed back against the pillows in an effort to escape any physical contact with him. "It's just a game with you," she said quietly. "You know a lot about women and you can tie me in knots without really trying, and you enjoy taunting me with it. But I'm not a toy, Clint, I'm a human being, and I don't like being... used!"

He stared at her without any expression

at all in his dark face. "You thought I was...playing, Maggie?" he asked.

Her eyes riveted themselves on the silken knot of his tie. "I should never have come," she said softly, regret in her tone. "That summer I made a fool of myself is still there, like a curtain you like to pull down often enough that I'll never forget what I did. Don't you think," she asked bitterly, "that I've been punished enough, Clint?"

"I'll agree with you on one point," he said curtly. "You shouldn't have come. Why I let myself be talked into it..."

"I'll be gone in another week," she reminded him.

"Back to what?" he asked then, his eyes narrow and assessing. "Back to the two-timing boyfriend? Back to your old job in his office?"

Her lower lip trembled. "Where I go and what I do is none of your business, Clint Raygen!"

His smile was mocking. "Thank God," he replied.

She sighed heavily. "You are, without a doubt, the most maddening man I've ever known!"

"So you're going to run out on me," he taunted. "Leave me here with no secretary and no prospects of finding one before you leave."

"You said two weeks," she reminded him narrowly.

"Make it four."

"Clint..."

"Just until Janna comes, little girl," he said quietly.

She avoided his eyes. "You don't want me here."

"No, I don't," he said, suddenly serious, "and remind me one day to tell you why—in about five years."

"Is it going to take that long to make up an answer?" she asked pertly.

He studied her face for a long time. "No," he said finally, "but it looks like it's going to take that long for you to grow up enough to understand the answer."

"Will you still be around then, you poor old doddering thing?" she asked in mock innocence.

His hands caught her face and held it in a vise-like grip on the pillow. "You damned little irritating cat, will you stop throwing my age at me?"

"Turn about's fair play," she said sweetly. "You take every opportunity to remind me of mine."

"And you've never stopped to wonder why, have you?" he growled.

She pushed against his hard chest. "Don't you have a plane or bus or train or something to catch?" she muttered.

His lips made a thin line as he glared down at her. "Can I trust you not to pull any more harebrained stunts until I get back?"

"Harebrained?" she replied hotly. "And just who upset me in the first place...!"

"If you hadn't panicked while I was making love to you..."

"You were *not*...!" she gasped.

His thumb pressed against her lips, stopping the indignant protest. "I would have been," he said quietly, "if you hadn't chickened out."

Her eyes flashed up at him. She jerked her face aside. "You flatter yourself that I'd have let you!" she returned.

"Or Philip?" he asked quietly. His eyes narrowed at the color in her cheeks. "I don't think I've ever known a woman as chaste as you are. You're so damned afraid of anything physical, Maggie, that I thought it was coldness for a long time, but it isn't. You're afraid to let go with a man."

"Am I?" she returned calmly, careful not to let him see how close to the truth he was. "Or is it soothing to your pride to think I am?"

"You little brat!" he growled, and, leaning forward, he caught her face in long, merciless fingers, spearing them into the hair at her temples to hold her. "Was it too close to the truth, Maggie?"

Her hands went up against his chest, pushing at it helplessly. "Let go of me! You think you know so much...!"

The fingers holding her head suddenly released it to catch her wrists like traps and slam them up over her head, pinning them to the bed.

There was something strangely ruthless in the way he looked down at her struggling, twisting body, in the burning half-smile that flamed on his chiseled mouth. "Fight me, wildcat," he murmured in a dangerous, low tone. "I love it when you fight...!"

She twisted instinctively, but his body went down to half cover hers, pressing her slenderness into the mattress, leaving only her eyes free to struggle.

The look on his dark face frightened her almost as much as the green fires that burned deep in his eyes, as he looked down at her with something like triumph. His glittery gaze shifted to her parted, trembling mouth.

"Don't!" she protested shakily as his dark head moved down.

He only laughed, softly, confidently. "Try being a woman instead of a cowering child," he said against her soft mouth as he took it.

An outraged cry broke from her under the punishing force of the kiss. She was aware of struggling briefly, fighting him until she felt the sting of his teeth against her soft lips, until the warm, steely nearness burned through the bedclothes against her, until he forced her trembling mouth to part for him and taught her sensations she'd never been capable of feeling.

She began to relax involuntarily when his mouth eased its pressure and became caressing, seductive, arousing. He released her wrists and his warm, long-fingered hands came down to cup her face, tilting it gently as he deepened the kiss in an intimacy she'd never shared with a man. A soft, barely audible protest broke from her.

"Not yet," he murmured deeply, his breath mingling with hers as he nipped sensuously at the soft contours of her mouth. "Kiss me back."

Her wet lashes opened lazily over misty, confused eyes, to find him staring back at her. He was so close that she could see the tiny lines around his eyelids, the dark eyebrows above them. Wonderingly, her fingers went up to trace them down to the hint of a frown that wrinkled his brow.

He drew back slowly, studying her. Her mouth was parted, her hair wild and disheveled, her eyes shimmering with mingled pleasure and awe.

"Beautiful little cat," he murmured, and his breath came heavily with the words. His hands slid into the thick tangle of hair at her ears, gently caressing. "Your eyes are like emeralds. I like the way you feel under me, Maggie."

Her lips parted as she tried to catch her

breath, her heart racing under the warm crush of his chest. "You...hurt me," she whispered.

"That's what it's all about, little girl," he said quietly. His mouth brushed hers tenderly. "You bit me," he whispered against the moist, bruised softness.

She sighed against the drugging brush of his warm mouth, drowning in pleasure. "You...you bit me back," she murmured.

He laughed softly. "With a vengeance. I was afraid I'd drawn blood," he mused, studying the bruised little mouth so close under his. "I've never fought so damned hard for a kiss."

Her lips pouted up at him, her eyes clouding. "Well, don't think I enjoyed it!" she muttered.

"Didn't you, honey?" he asked deeply, and leaned down to tease her mouth with his in a heady, coaxing pressure that tore a moan from her throat as she raised up against him in a silent plea.

But he drew away and stood up in a

smooth, graceful motion to bend a calculating gaze down at her. His dark hair was ruffled, his mouth sensuous from the contact with hers. The silk tie was disarranged, and he looked altogether masculine and disturbing.

He turned away to straighten his tie and his hair in her mirror. "What are you going to do while I'm gone?" he asked carelessly.

She fought to regain her composure, clutching the bedclothes around her as if they were a lifeline. "Work, I suppose. Did...did you leave any letters you want done?"

"Not a word," he replied coolly. He pulled a cigarette out of his pocket and lit it. "Take another day or so before you start back into the routine, little one. I don't want you to have a relapse."

She rubbed her bruised arms and wrists gingerly, darting an accusing glance his way. "That concern is a little late, isn't it?"

He smiled rakishly. "Did I bruise you?" he asked without a trace of sympathy in his deep voice.

"Yes!"

"And you loved every second of it, you little hypocrite," he taunted. "I'm almost sorry I stopped. Another few minutes and you'd have been clawing my back to ribbons."

She gasped at the insinuation. "How dare you!"

"You sound like something out of a very old Victorian novel," he observed, mischief in every line of his face. "Did it shock you that you could feel that kind of violent emotion with a man, Maggie—violent enough to make you bite and claw?"

She dropped her eyes like hot irons, concentrating on the clasped hands on the bedcovers. "It wasn't like that," she whispered. "I was fighting you, not..."

"I hope you'll remember this the next time you decide to use those formidable young hands on me," he remarked.

"What do you mean?" she grumbled.

He caught her eyes with a narrow, level gaze, and there was no humor in it. "I want you," he said bluntly, with no warning. "I don't take much encouragement, either, and that's something you'd better remember. You're not the little girl I used to carry around on my shoulders anymore. You're a woman, and you feel like a woman, and, God, I like touching you!"

She blushed to her toes. "If you think I'd let you…!"

"You just did," he countered.

"You didn't…touch me!" she flashed.

"We both know I could have," he said patiently. "You fought me like a tigress at first, I'll give you that. But you didn't stop me, did you?"

She glared at him, but she didn't deny it. She couldn't.

He took a long draw from his cigarette and studied her through narrowed eyes. "I never thought there was any danger of this happening, but I've just found out how wrong I was. Watch yourself, little girl. I know a hell of a lot more about it than you do, and I'm not above using every dirty trick in the book when I'm aroused. No man is.''

She avoided his glance. ''You always used to say I didn't affect you like that,'' she told the bedcovers.

''Honey, you're not any more shocked about it than I am,'' he replied tightly. ''I was just teasing you that day by the stream, the same way I'd been teasing you ever since you came here. But when I laid you down under that tree, and felt that soft mouth under mine for the first time... My God, Maggie,'' he breathed, ''if you hadn't drawn your hand back when you did, if it hadn't just happened to hit me the wrong way...'' His eyes narrowed as he moved to stand beside the bed, looking down at her broodingly. ''You little fool, couldn't you feel my hands trembling, or did you just not know what it meant?''

She ducked her head so that the cloud

of dark hair hid her face from him. "I didn't know what it meant," she admitted miserably.

"I'm not trying to embarrass you, little innocent," he said gently. "I'm not trying to seduce you, either, but I'm not immune to you. Maggie, you're not the kind of woman a man uses. You were meant for a white wedding and children—and those things have no place in my life. You know that, don't you?"

She nodded. "I've always known it, Clint," she said quietly. "You've never made any secret of the way you felt about marriage."

"I don't like being tied down," he said harshly through a veil of smoke. "I can't bear possession, Maggie. In plain language, I've never found a woman I wanted that much, and I've never loved one. It isn't in me."

Her eyes shot to his face. "I don't remember proposing to you," she said.

He chuckled, the seriousness gone from

his dark face. "It's just as well, Irish. We'd kill each other the first week."

"Amen." She traced the pattern on the bedspread. "For what it's worth, I don't like possession, either. Or being bullied," she added impishly.

He was quiet for a long moment. "Then why were you marrying Philip?"

"He didn't dominate me."

"Didn't, or couldn't?" he challenged. "Could you lead him around by the nose? Was that the attraction?"

"You go to hell!" she told him.

He only smiled, his lips mocking her. "You're going to take a lot of taming," he said speculatively. "I almost envy the man who'll get to do it."

Only a man like Clint, though, would enjoy it, she thought, would look on it as a challenge and make of it a pleasure that even imagination couldn't do justice to.

"The right man wouldn't have to fight me," she murmured defensively.

His face was quiet, solemn, as he searched hers. "What a waste," he said gently. "I don't like you submissive, Margaretta Leigh."

"How would you know?" she challenged. "You've never seen me that way!"

His eyes narrowed. "I don't think I'd want to," he replied quietly. "You're fierce when you fight, Irish. I think you'd love a man just as fiercely. Submission from you would be like possessing a wax doll." His eyes dropped to her full lips. "I'd like to feel that soft mouth on fire with passion just one time."

Her eyes fought him. "You won't," she threw at him. "Not ever!"

"Don't bet on it," he murmured softly, and she felt her heart stop at the look in his eyes when he said it. He turned and opened the door, glancing back at the picture she made. "Miss me."

"Please, hold your breath waiting for me to." She smiled sarcastically.

"Stay away from the horses while I'm gone," he returned, and, with a wink, he went out, closing the door firmly behind him.

With a cry of rage, she buried her face in the pillow.

Seven

Several days later—his few, plus some—she was back on her feet and too restless to sit still. Walking idly in the pecan grove under a spreading canopy of natural arches, she wondered how it was possible to miss a man so much. Most of her life had been spent away from Clint, but it had never hurt like this. Perhaps, she admitted quietly, because it had only been infatuation before. A wanting that had nothing to do with reality, but had sprung from her girlish daydreams about him. Daydreams that had gone up in smoke at the first touch of his mouth.

It wasn't infatuation anymore. She wanted him in a way that terrified her. Not just to sit and hero-worship, but to fight with, and work with, and love with for the rest of her life.

Her pale green eyes sought the horizon far in the distance. Where was he now? Who was he with? Was there a woman somewhere who could reach that proud, stubborn heart of his and make it throb with longing? She sighed, remembering the sultry look in his eyes when she'd yielded to him. She'd never seen that look on his face before, that dark, masculine triumph mingled with a hunger that was just as exciting in memory as it had been in reality. Clint had wanted her. But wanting wasn't loving. And she wondered miserably if Clint even knew the definition of love.

It was inevitable that she'd wind up by the little stream with its curtain of long, curling gray Spanish moss dangling lazily from the tall oak trees at the bank's edge.

With a sigh, her eyes went to the carpet of twigs and fallen leaves under that massive oak where Clint had...

Her eyes closed on the memory, hearing again the deep, soft voice in her ear, feeling the delicious crush of his arms, the slow, confident experience in the mouth that had taught hers what a kiss should be.

Her eyes misted with remembrance as she studied the leaf-covered ground that bore no trace of two enemies who had behaved almost like lovers here. If only. She sighed again, reaching up to touch the moss as her eyes followed the bubbling stream where it wound like a silver ribbon into the distance between the leafy trees. Oh, if only!

She had to leave. She knew it suddenly and surely. If she stayed here now, knowing the way she felt, she'd have no defense at all against him if he touched her again. Despite the promise she'd made to stay until Janna came, she'd have to leave. She was more vulnerable now than she'd ever been. And, she admitted to herself, Clint wouldn't hesitate to test that vulnerability. He'd always known—or thought he did— exactly how she felt about him. He seemed to enjoy the power he had over her. And now…

She turned back toward the house. She didn't have a choice anymore.

Surprisingly, almost as if Janna could read her mind, she called that night after supper.

"How's it going?" Janna asked, and Maggie could almost see the grin on her friend's face.

"How do you think it's going?" she asked. "Janna, I love you like a sister, but I'm going to poison you when I get back."

"Oh," she sighed. "I'd hoped from what Brent said…"

"You talked to Brent?" Maggie burst out. "But he's in Hong Kong…?"

"Hong Kong! Brent?"

Puzzle pieces whirled around in her mind. "But Clint said…"

"My sweet brother threatened to break his arms if he came back down there while you were in residence," Janna said triumphantly.

There was a long, static silence while Maggie tried to fit the puzzle pieces together into something that made sense. "I don't understand," she muttered absently.

"I do. You and Brent were always close, weren't you? Maggie, my dear," Janna said gently, "don't you know that my brother doesn't tolerate competition from anybody? If he wants something badly enough, he'll use some of the most ruthless methods in the book to get it. And apparently," she added with smug pleasure, "what he wants right now is you."

Boy, if you only knew, Maggie thought. "Been eating green toadstools again, huh,

Janna?'' she asked pleasantly. "The only thing going on between Clint and me is one everlasting argument, and this time we've very nearly come to blows. All I want is to go home. When are you coming down here?''

There was a wistful sigh on the other end of the line. "Saturday,'' came the reply. "Or maybe Friday night, I'm not sure. I had my vacation switched. If you're determined, we can go back to Columbus next week.''

"Determined isn't the word. Oh, Janna, come protect me,'' she moaned. "I'm so tired of fighting...''

"Are you well, Maggie?'' her friend asked. "You, tired of fighting Clint? That's got to be a first.''

"It'll make all the record books, but I really am. Hurry, will you?''

"All right, since it's you asking. But, Maggie, why did Clint threaten to break both of Brent's arms?''

"Because we stole his rotor, tied bows

on his cows' tails, and I filled the swimming pool with a box of bubble bath or two..."

"Never mind, and I thought it was something romantic. Can you stay out of trouble until I get there, Maggie?"

"Nothing easier," she laughed. "Clint's still gone, and all I have to do is keep out of his way until you get here."

It was late afternoon when Maggie delivered Emma's grocery list to Shorty, and she paused on the front porch to feast her eyes on the fiery sunset with its blazing fingers of color before she went inside. The city had nothing, she thought, to compare with this. The sweep of open land, the smell of country air laced with the smell of flowers, the sound of dogs barking in the distance, the peace of nonmechanical sounds. And Clint had called her a city girl. She shook her head as she went into the house. He didn't know her at all.

She walked into the study and, unexpectedly, he was there. It was like being hit in the stomach with a baseball bat. She felt her heart stop just at the sight of him. He looked as though he'd just gotten home, still dressed in a dark brown suit and a cream silk shirt. He turned and gazed at her, something dark and strange and violent flashing in his eyes at the sight of her standing there in the little yellow polka-dotted sundress she'd thrown on in a whim. He sketched her quietly, deliberately, pausing at the low bodice, the thin straps that left her round, smooth shoulders bare, her hair hanging silkily around them.

"H...hello," she stammered, captured by his narrow eyes.

"Hello," he replied. "Going somewhere?"

"Oh...the dress, you mean?" She shook her head. "I...it got hot."

"It's getting hotter by the minute," he mused, and his eyes went from her wavy dark hair to her sandals.

She swallowed nervously at the sensuous, masculine appreciation in his eyes. "How...how was your trip?"

His face seemed to go taut at the question. He turned away to light a cigarette and take a deep draw before he replied, "Not very pleasant, little girl. I swung by Austin to see Masterson."

"Duke?" She felt something dark stir inside her, something cold and ominous. "How was he?"

"I got there in time for the funeral," he said quietly.

The unexpected blow brought tears to her eyes as she remembered the big, dark man and ancient tombs and the lure of the past all at once in a jumble of thoughts. "Oh," she whispered brokenly.

He turned with a heavy sigh. "His plane crashed on the way back home," he told her. "In a way, it was a blessing. He was in a hell of a lot of pain. And to have to wait for it..."

She nodded silently, agreeing that it was best, while inside she felt as if something had been torn out of her. Tears ran un-ashamedly down her face.

His eyes darkened. "For God's sake, stop it!" he growled. "Masterson wouldn't want that. He wouldn't want you to grieve for him!"

She bit her lip, hating him for being so insensitive, so cold. "Excuse me," she said brokenly. "Caring is the number one sin in your book of rules, isn't it?"

She turned and started toward the door. He caught her before she went two steps, whipping her around into his hard arms, pressing her shaken, trembling body close against the warm strength of his.

"I can't bear to watch you cry," he murmured harshly against her temple. His fingers contracted in the cloud of hair at her nape.

The admission stunned her until she re-alized that, like most men, he couldn't stand tears from any source. She fought to regain her composure, to stop the hot tears from running down her face into the corners of her mouth.

"I liked him," she said unsteadily. "It was as if...as if I'd known him all my life."

"It happens that way sometimes." His arms contracted, and she felt one warm, lean hand against her bare back just above the line of her sundress, gently caressing the silky skin. Under her ear she could feel the sudden heavy sigh of his breath as his lips brushed against her forehead, and she stiffened involuntarily.

He drew back abruptly, his hand going to the inside pocket of his jacket. "Masterson had this in his pocket," he said, handing her an unsealed envelope. "It was addressed to you. His nephew asked me to deliver it."

She swallowed nervously, staring at the small white envelope in her hand, at the bold, black scrawl of her name and the ranch's address. "For me? What...what is it?"

"I don't know," he said, moving away from her to retrieve his smoking cigarette from the ashtray on his desk. "None of us felt we had the right to read it."

She fingered it with a sigh. She couldn't bring herself to open it here, now, with Clint only a few feet away. "I'll read it later. Clint, Janna called. She's coming Saturday."

He whirled on his heels, his eyes narrow, his face harsh. "Did you call for reinforcements?" he demanded hotly.

"No!" she flashed. "She called and said she was coming. What was I supposed to do? Tell her no, and that her brother...?"

"That her brother what?" he growled.

She turned away. "I left all your messages on the desk," she said quietly.

There was a long pause. "I bought some replacement heifers," he said finally, the iron control back in his deep voice. "And a couple of bulls to add to my breeding stock. We'll get those records out of the way tomorrow."

"Yes," she said in a whisper.

"Maggie."

She paused with her hand on the doorknob, but she didn't turn around to face him. "What?"

"Don't wear that dress again."

She was afraid to ask him why. The husky note in his voice was almost answer enough.

Upstairs, in the privacy of her room, she sat down in a chair by the darkened window and read her letter by the light of the small lamp.

Margaretta Leigh, it began in a thick, heavy masculine hand, *if I'd had more time to arrange it, I'd have sent you a ticket to Stonehenge instead. As it is, I was holding this one for a free week which, in all honesty, I'm not expecting to have. You'll find that all the expenses are covered, from the cruise to meals and lodging. I had to get home in a hurry, or I'd have twisted your arm and made you take this ticket. Maggie, please don't refuse it. Humor an old man who enjoyed a few of the happiest hours of his life in your company. It was almost like a homecoming. I don't know if you believe in déjà vu,* the letter continued, and she shivered involuntarily, *but if such things happen, maybe we knew each other in some distant past and shared more than coffee and conversation. This lifetime wasn't for us. Maybe next time. With deep affection, Duke Masterson.*

Maybe next time... Her eyes closed as she folded the letter back around the ticket. When the tears passed, she read the letter over again and stared at the ticket. It was for a round trip passage to archaeological sites all over the Mediterranean, all expenses paid, on a cruise which was to begin the following Monday. She stared blankly at it. Could she really afford to go now, when she should be looking for a job...

Emma's voice calling her to supper

stopped the confusing thoughts temporarily.

It plagued her, whether or not to go on the cruise. She wanted to, desperately. But she was torn between pleasure and the very real problem of a job to go to when she left the ranch. She hadn't told anybody about the ticket. It was safely put away in her purse, tucked in Duke's letter, and she kept it secretly like a prayer too precious to share with anyone. But she was troubled, and it showed.

She felt Clint's brooding eyes on her at breakfast the day before Janna was due home. He watched her like a hawk these days, she thought bitterly, even though he'd been careful to keep as far away from her as possible ever since he came back from his trip. The way he avoided her had even raised Emma's eyebrows, no mean feat. Maggie was at once hurt and relieved by it. At least she didn't have to fight any monstrous temptations. There weren't any.

"Why don't you talk about it," Clint

growled finally when she'd finished picking at the eggs and bacon on her plate, "instead of sitting there with that damned crucified look on your face?"

Her eyes burned as her face jerked up. "Why don't you mind your own business?"

"You are my business," he said shortly.

"Not for much longer."

"Praise God!"

She threw down her napkin and stormed out past Emma who was just coming in with a plate full of ham. "Maggie...?" she called.

Clint went right out the door behind her, his jaw set, his eyes blazing.

"Clint...?" Emma murmured.

Neither one of them seemed to even hear her. With a sigh and a shrug, she took the ham back to the kitchen.

Clint caught up to Maggie on the front porch, jerking her around with a rough, cruel hand.

"Stop throwing tantrums," he said

gruffly, "or I'll give you my cure for them."

She tossed her hair impatiently. "Please let go of my arm."

"Where are you going?"

"For a ride! Is that all right, or do I have to…?"

He pressed a long, gentle finger against her lips, reading the emotional storm that was tearing at her as he met her eyes.

"No more," he said softly. "Come riding with me. It'll help."

She gazed up at him helplessly, feeling the yielding start and hating it. "Aren't…aren't you busy?"

"Always, honey," he said with a kind smile.

"I…I can go alone," she murmured.

"I want to be with you," he said. His lean hand brushed some stray hairs away from her lips. "We haven't had much time together since I've been home."

"You wanted it that way," she replied, hiding her eyes from him.

"I know."

"Clint…" Her eyes went up to meet his, a question in them.

He shook his head. "Not now. Not yet." His dark brows drew together as he looked down at her, as if she made a puzzle he couldn't put together. "Damn it, woman…!"

Her lower lip trembled at the sudden anger. "What have I done now?" she grumbled.

He drew a sharp breath and turned away. "Never mind. Come on!"

They rode in a companionable silence for several minutes, and Maggie knew that she'd treasure this time with him like a hoard of gold when she left the ranch. Her eyes darted toward him when he wasn't looking at her, tracing the sharp profile, the powerful set of his shoulders, the straight back. The sight of him was like a cold drink in the desert. She wished she'd brought her camera, that she could have a picture of him to take home and… She sighed. She'd carry a picture of him in her heart until the day she died. That would be haunting enough.

"What are you thinking about?" he asked her after a while.

"The memories," she sighed, smiling at the sweep of open country as they reined up and sat quietly on their mounts, side by side. "So many of them. The meadow where Janna and I used to pick wildflowers, the pecan trees that had such delicious fat pecans on them in the fall, the..."

"The stream where I made love to you?"

She glared at him, blushing, her eyes on the brim of his hat, pulled low and shading his glittery eyes.

"Were you always that conceited, or did you have to work at it?" she returned.

"You make me conceited, little girl," he replied sharply. "My God, if you'd reacted to your poor fool of a fiancé the way you react to me physically, you'd still be engaged!"

She clamped her teeth together and ignored him.

He threw his leg over the pommel of his saddle while he lit a cigarette. He shoved the brim back over his eyes, and they burned into her face even at that distance, green and fiery and strange.

"How was it, Maggie?" he asked with a deep, low whip in his voice. "How did it feel to kiss me? You'd wanted it since you were sixteen. Was it worth the daydreaming?"

She studied her trembling hands on the reins, hardly believing the nightmare the ride had turned into.

He took a long draw from the cigarette. "No comeback? Maybe I disappointed you," he continued mercilessly, his eyes narrowing. "Infatuation doesn't stand up to the demands a man can make on a woman, does it, little one? Any more than dreams stand up to reality. What a hell of a pity you didn't realize that four summers ago."

"Amen," she whispered through her teeth. "Was that what…"

He laughed, and the harsh sound hurt more than the words had. "I couldn't think of a better way to cure you, honey. I'd had about all the hero worship I could stand. I did us both a favor."

"Thanks," she said in a pale whisper. "Coming on the heels of my broken engagement, it was just what I needed."

"You're breaking my heart."

"You don't have one!" she shot back, her eyes burning with unshed tears as she glared at him. "You wouldn't know what to do with it if you had one."

He shrugged, putting the cigarette back to his chiseled lips. "Maybe," he replied quietly. "But you'd better thank your lucky stars that I have a conscience, young lady," he added pointedly. "I could have had you."

It was the truth, and it hurt like hell, and she closed her eyes on the pain and the shame.

"Infatuation or not, you wanted me!" he growled, leashed fury in every line of his face.

"To my everlasting shame," she whispered brokenly. Her eyes when they met his were bright with tears and hurt.

His face went stone-hard, as if she'd slapped him.

"I'm leaving in the morning, Janna or no Janna," she whispered huskily. "I've been tortured by you enough for one lifetime!"

She whirled the mare and urged her into a gallop as she headed blindly back to the house, leaning forward in the saddle as if devils were in hot pursuit. But Clint wasn't following her. He was sitting frozen in his saddle, his eyes blank and unseeing as smoke trailed from the forgotten cigarette in his hand.

Supper was an ordeal, and Maggie wouldn't have felt the slightest twinge of conscience about missing it if it hadn't been for Emma.

She didn't look toward Clint at all through the meal, or speak to him. Emma, caught in the middle, tried to keep the conversation going with a monologue of comments about the weather, the government, and the Napoleonic Wars. But it was a lost cause. Neither of them even looked up.

Maggie helped clear the table while Clint stormed off into his den and closed the door behind him with a force that rattled windows.

"Is it because you're leaving tomorrow?" Emma asked as they washed up.

"I don't know." She dried a plate and set it aside. "We had an argument while we were out riding."

"You've had arguments since you were eight years old, missie, but he didn't ever slam doors before or leave good coffee sitting in his cup without even tasting it." Emma looked at her pleadingly. "Maggie, don't go. Not like this."

"You don't understand, Emma, I have to," she said miserably.

"Why? Because you're afraid he'll make you give in?"

Her face jerked up, astonishment in her pale eyes.

"Oh, yes, I know," Emma said gently. "It's written all over both of you. Don't you know why he got Brent away from here? Why he can't take his eyes off you lately?"

She lowered her eyes to the soapy water in the sink. "I can't give him what he wants."

"Do you know what he wants, Maggie? Does he?"

"Oh, yes," she replied bitterly. "He wants me to find someone else to 'hero-worship.'"

"Isn't that odd," Emma remarked, "when he never seemed to mind it before?"

Maggie attacked another plate with the drying cloth.

"Stay one more day," Emma coaxed.

"Janna's going to be here in the morning and everything will be better. You'll see."

"Emma…!"

"Take him his coffee."

"And get my head snapped off?"

The older woman touched her hand gently. "Maggie, you can't let this drag on any longer. It's tearing you both apart. Take him his coffee, talk to him. I think… Maggie, I think he's hurt more than he's angry."

"You couldn't hurt him with a bomb. He's invulnerable," she growled.

"Go on."

She gave Emma a last resentful glance and, with a reluctant sigh, picked up the mug of hot coffee and took it into the study.

It was like facing a lion on his home ground, she thought, as she walked in after his gruff, "Come in!" She pushed the door shut behind her and carried the coffee to his big oak desk. He was standing outside on the patio, his shoulder against the doorjamb, a smoking cigarette in his hand.

He turned to watch her set the cup down, and she almost caught her breath at the sheer masculinity that seemed to radiate from his tall, powerful body. His shirt was unbuttoned against the heat, hanging loosely from his broad shoulders, revealing a thick mat of curling dark hair that made a wedge against the smooth bronze muscles of his chest and stomach. His thick hair was tousled, as if his fingers had restlessly worked in it. His eyes were narrow and solemn and darker than she'd ever seen them.

"I...Emma said to...to bring your coffee to you," she faltered, the words coming unsteadily as he shouldered away from the door and started toward her.

"Where's yours?" he asked quietly.

"Mine?"

"You could have had it with me."

"Oh." She studied the carpet. "I...I had mine in the kitchen."

He perched on the edge of the desk and crushed out the finished cigarette.

"I don't want it to be like this," she whispered miserably. "I don't want to leave here with you hating me…!"

"I don't hate you," he replied deeply.

No, she thought, because that required emotion and there wasn't any in him. He was simply indifferent.

She studied her shoes. "Anyway," she said quietly, "thanks for letting me come. I'm sorry to leave you without a secretary…"

"You aren't," he said coolly. "I ran into Lida while I was away. The marriage broke up overnight. She'll be here Monday." He smiled carelessly. "So you see, little girl, you picked a good time to go. No harm done."

She smiled brightly despite the throbbing ache in her heart. "No harm done," she echoed. "Well, I'll say goodnight…"

"Take this back with you." He drained the mug and handed it to her. But as their fingers touched, he felt the cold trembling of hers and something seemed to explode in his eyes.

"Cool as ice," he murmured through set lips. "But only on the outside." His hand whipped out and caught her by the shoulder, dragging her to him. In this half-sitting position, she was on an unnerving level with his jade eyes. "You don't like me to know just how much I affect you, do you, Irish?" he growled angrily.

"Don't..." she pleaded, all the fight gone out of her at the merciless fury she read in his eyes. "Clint, please, let me go, don't..."

"Don't what? Shame you?" he taunted. He snatched the cup out of her hands and tossed it onto the desk. His lean hands gripped her shoulders fiercely, slamming her against him.

"Clint, I'm sorry!" she whispered, realizing at last what was wrong. She'd stung his pride, and now he wanted revenge...

"You don't know what shame is," he growled, bending his head, "but I'm going to teach you."

"Clint...!" Her voice broke on the pleading cry, just as his hard mouth went down against hers and taught her what a punishment a kiss could be.

She tried to struggle against the merciless hard arms that held her, but she couldn't get loose, she couldn't breathe...yielding to the strength that was so much greater than her own.

Then, like magic, the crush of his muscular arms eased, cradling her now as gently as he'd hurt her before. The pressure of his mouth lessened, became soft and caressing, coaxing.

"Maggie," he whispered against her bruised lips, sliding his hands under the hem of her blouse to burn against the bare flesh of her back. "Maggie, you feel like silk."

Her fingers curled into the cotton of his shirt as she hung there, breathless, while he toyed with her mouth, taunting it with brief, biting kisses that kindled fires in her mind. His lean, warm hands pressed her even closer, rasping slightly as they brushed her smooth skin.

"Touch me," he murmured huskily. "Touch me, honey."

Involuntarily, her slender hands moved away from the cotton shirt onto the warm, bronzed muscles of his broad chest, tangling in the thick cushion of curling black hair as she caressed him blindly, feeling the sensuous masculinity of him, drowning in the tangy scent of his cologne as sensation after sensation washed over her.

"Like that, hellcat," he murmured, "that's it. Maggie, open your mouth, just a little. I want to taste it…"

Burning with the hunger he created in her, she yielded mindlessly as he opened her soft lips and drew her completely against the long, warm body, building the pressure until he heard the moan smothered under his mouth.

"Did that milksop fiancé of yours ever kiss you like this, Maggie?" he growled huskily. "Did he stir you until you moaned against his mouth?"

"Oh, don't," she pleaded dizzily, her slender hands making a halfhearted protest against the pleasure his were causing.

"Why not? You want it," he whispered. His mouth brushed lazily over hers, open and moist and deliberately sensuous. "You want my hands and my eyes on every inch of this sweet young body, don't you, Maggie? Answer me. *Don't you*!"

Her voice broke on a sob. "Yes!" she wept. "Damn you, yes!"

"Ask me nice and sweet, Maggie," he taunted. "Say, please Clint, say it, Irish. Whisper it..."

Her eyes opened slowly, bright with longing and love. "Please," she breathed against his hard, torturing mouth. "Please, Clint..."

His hands contracted on her waist as he suddenly thrust her roughly away. A cold, merciless smile tugged at his mouth. "And that, Miss Kirk, evens the score. You wanted something to be ashamed of. You've got it!"

It took seconds for her to realize what he'd said, what he'd done. Her face went red, then white. Deathly white. Ashamed of...even the score... She gaped at him numbly, feeling as though she'd been slammed with all the strength in that tanned, lean hand.

He lit a cigarette calmly, his narrow eyes flicking her stunned expression as he snapped the lighter shut and pocketed it. "You've been following me around like a damned pet dog since you were about eight years old," he remarked. "For future reference, I'm tired of it. I won't be a stand-in for a jilting fiancé, or a balm for a broken heart. From now on, if you want to be made love to, look in some other direction. I'm tired of giving you lessons."

Her face went, if possible, even whiter. Her mouth refused to form the words that would tell him how hateful she thought he was. Inside, she felt beaten, bruised. Tears misted on her long lashes, tears that she turned away to keep him from seeing. She went blindly toward the door.

"No comeback, Maggie?" he chided.

Her hand touched the doorknob.

"Would you like me to kiss you good-bye?" he persisted.

She opened the door and went out.

"Irish!"

She closed the door behind her and went blindly and quickly up the steps. Behind her she was vaguely aware of the door opening again, of eyes following her. But she didn't slow down or look back. Not once.

Eight

Maggie sat in the chair by her bed in the dark for hours, aching with a hurt that went deeper than any pain. The deliberate cruelty was almost unbearable. He knew he'd hurt her. She'd seen the satisfaction in his jade eyes. And all because she'd stung his ego. For no other reason than that.

The tears hadn't stopped since she closed the door behind her into this womb of security that was darkness. Hadn't stopped, hadn't eased. Not when the knock came hesitantly on the door and Emma's voice called her name gently. Not when she heard two voices outside the locked room, one deep and slow and angry, the other soft and pleading.

When the first light of dawn filtered through the fluffy white curtains, she still hadn't moved from the chair, or slept. Her eyes were red-rimmed and dark shadowed, her face as white as it had been last night.

Automatically, she began to pack, quietly and efficiently stuffing clean and dirty clothes together in the single suitcase, gathering cosmetics from the chest of drawers, her toiletries from the bathroom. She didn't allow herself to think. Not about what she'd felt for Clint, not about what he'd done to her, not about the anguish of walking away from him for the rest of her life. She kept her mind on getting away and nothing else. Escape was the only important thing left in her life right now. She wanted to run.

Without pausing to drag a brush through her hair, she picked up the case and, without a backward glance, closed the door.

"Oh, there you are," Emma said in a strange, hesitant tone as Maggie reached the bottom of the staircase. "Ready for breakfast, missie? Surely you're not going to leave without breakfast?"

Maggie didn't answer, making do with a short, wordless shake of her head. She picked up the phone and calmly called a taxi, aware as she put the receiver down that Clint had come into the hall.

Emma exchanged a quick glance with him and left the hallway, quietly closing the kitchen door behind her with a soft click.

Maggie picked up her case and started for the front porch just as Clint moved, standing quietly in front of her, his hands jammed deep into the pockets of his jeans. His own eyes were bloodshot, his face haggard. She only spared him a brief, cold glance before she averted her eyes.

"Please get out of my way," she said in an uncommonly quiet tone.

"I want to talk to you, Maggie."

"Write me a letter," she said to her shoes. "If you try, you can probably come up with a few more insults by the time you mail it."

"Maggie!" he groaned, reaching out to touch her shoulder.

She flinched away from him as if he'd cut her to the bone, backing away with wide, burning eyes. "Don't ever do that again," she whispered unsteadily. "Don't ever touch me. I'm getting out of your life just as quickly as I can, Clint, isn't that enough?" Tears misted in her eyes. "What more do you want from me, blood?" she cried.

He drew a deep, slow breath. "My God, I never meant to hurt you..." he breathed huskily, something dark and somber in his eyes as they searched her face.

"No, you didn't, did you?" she asked bitterly. "You wanted to take the hide off Lida, but she wasn't here and I was. Maybe things will look up now, since she's coming back."

"Maggie, not like this, for God's sake!" he growled as she started for the door. "I want to tell you…!"

"The score's even, Clint, you said so," she told him from the porch, her eyes accusing. "There's nothing more you can say that I want to hear. You said it all last night."

His eyes narrowed as if in pain, his gaze searching, quiet, as if he'd never seen her before and couldn't get enough of her face. "No, honey," he said gently. "I didn't say enough. Maggie…"

A loud blare from a car horn coming up the driveway interrupted him, and she turned and started down the steps with a burst of relief that made her slender shoulders slump. "Tell Emma goodbye," she called over her shoulder, "and tell Janna I'll write!"

He didn't answer her, his face dark and still, his eyes riveted to the slender form as it crawled into the cab and the door closed. He watched her go, his eyes haunted and tortured as the cab slowly faded to a yellow speck in the distance.

Emma came out onto the porch behind him, drying her hands on the white apron.

"I've got breakfast," she said gently.

He didn't answer her, his eyes blank, his face drawn.

"You wanted her to go," Emma reminded him. "That's what you told me last night."

He turned and went into the house, into his den, closing the door behind him firmly. With a sigh, Emma went back to the kitchen, idly wondering how she was going to explain any of this to Janna.

Later, sitting wearily on the bus to Miami, Maggie read Duke Masterson's letter for the third time and said a silent thank you to the big dark man for this way out. She couldn't have borne going back to the apartment just yet, facing Janna and the inevitable questions. The wound was too raw, too new to be probed just now. In a few days, a few weeks...she gazed lovingly at the ticket that promised escape. It was a reprieve from too much hurting, too much pain. Philip, then Clint...especially Clint. She closed her eyes against the bitter memory. Would she ever forget how he'd humbled her; would she ever heal from the crippling blow her pride had suffered?

Her eyes turned to the window, to the palmettos and pines on the horizon, the occasional home tucked away in a nest of trees. Things were going to be awkward from now on. She wouldn't be able to spend holidays with Janna ever again if they meant the ranch and Clint. It would be worse when he flew into town on business and came to see his sister. She sighed wearily. Perhaps it would be better if she looked for a job in Atlanta and moved away from her childhood friend. That would be painful, too. But maybe, in the long run, it would be for the best.

She leaned her head back against the seat and closed her tired eyes. It seemed so long since she'd slept, since she'd felt any peace at all. Her mind was full of Clint, of the old days.

It seemed so long ago that she and Clint had sat on the porch swing together and talked about horses. Or went for long rides in the forest as she listened to his tales about the early days of Florida's exploration when canoes sailed down the Suwannee River on scouting trips.

He made the Sunshine State come alive for her. She could see the proud Spanish conquistadores tramping through the underbrush by the river. She could hear the drums of the proud, fierce Seminoles, who were never conquered by the United States government despite a series of three wars they fought between 1817 and 1858. She could picture the tall sailing ships that departed Florida's sandy coast, bound for the Indies or South America.

She sighed. Clint had liked her as a child. They'd been friends. But now he was an enemy, and all her tears wouldn't change that. Not after what he'd done to her. Her eyes closed with pain at the memory. Had that really been necessary, she wondered, the humiliation he'd caused? Why should it have upset him so, what she said while they were out riding, about being ashamed of what he could make her feel?

She shook her head idly. If he'd wanted to shame her, he'd accomplished that. But what puzzled her was the look on his face the next morning, the dark, hungry look in the green eyes that watched her leave the ranch. Had it been guilt in his eyes—or pain?

Her brows came together. She wondered what Janna would think when she got there; or would Clint even tell his sister the whole story? She hadn't mentioned that she was going to Miami. Nobody knew she had the cruise ticket. Clint and Emma had simply assumed that she was going home to Columbus.

Well, what difference did it make, she wondered, her eyes on the cloudy landscape outside the tinted bus window as the sunset made lovely flames in the sky. How quickly the day had passed, and soon the Miami skyline would come into view on the horizon. She shifted restlessly on the comfortable seat. Miami. Would any of them worry besides Emma and Janna? Well, she would mail Janna a postcard from Greece or Crete or wherever she landed. Janna and Emma, she corrected.

She got off the bus in Miami and took a cab to Miami Beach where Collins Avenue boasted almost wall to wall hotels. She gaped like a country girl at the sights and sounds of Miami Beach at night, drinking in the salt sea smell, the glorious fairyland colors of the night lights. There was no parking space available at the hotel she chose, so the driver let her out across the busy street and lifted out her suitcase.

"Watch the traffic, lady," he cautioned as he handed her the change from her fare.

She nodded and smiled. "Awesome, isn't it?" she laughed.

"Not after you've been here a while." He grinned as he drove away.

She lifted the suitcase, still smiling as she surveyed the bigness and richness of this man-made Mecca. In just hours, she'd be on that cruise ship heading out into the Atlantic. Leaving behind her worries, her heartaches, her obligations, just for a little while. She took a deep breath of warm sea air. Thank you, Duke Masterson, she said silently, feeling a twinge of sadness that the big, dark man wouldn't be somewhere in those ancient ruins waiting for her.

She started toward the hotel across the street, her mind far away, her eyes unseeing. She didn't notice the powerful car pulling away from the curb with a squealing of tires just a few meters away. Not until she felt the sudden impact and everything whirled down into a painful sickening blackness....

Sound came and went in vague snatches, from a great distance.

"...Several ribs broken, internal injuries. She's not responding."

"She's got to! My God, do something, anything! I don't give a damn what it costs!"

"We're going to do all we can, of course. But...she's not trying, you see. To live, I mean. The will to live can make the difference in cases like these."

The voices faded away, and then one of them came back, deep and slow, and she was dimly aware of fingers curling around hers, holding them, caressing them.

"Running out on me?" the voice growled. "Is that what you're trying to do, Maggie, run some more?"

Her eyes fluttered, her brows contracted.

Her head moved restlessly on the cool pillow.

"I...don't want...to," she whispered half-consciously.

"Don't want to what?"

"Live," she managed. "Hurts...too much."

"Dying's going to hurt more," came the short reply. "Because if you go, I'm coming, too. You won't escape me that way. So help me, God, I'll follow you! Do you hear me, Maggie?"

Her head tossed. "Leave me...alone!" she whispered painfully.

"Why the hell should I? You won't leave me alone."

The fingers tightened, and she felt or thought she felt a surge of emotion flowing through them, warming her, touching her, gently holding her to life.

She licked her dry, cracked lips. "Don't...let go," she murmured, clenching her hand around those strong fingers.

"I'll never let go, little girl. Hang on, sweetheart. Just hang on."

"Hang...on," she breathed, and the darkness came again.

The voices came and went again, now droning, now arguing. A feminine one joined in, pleading, soft. It was like a strange symphony of sound, mingled with the clanging of metallic objects, the coolness of sheets, the feel of warm water and cool hands. And that one voice...

"Don't give up now," it commanded, and she felt the strong fingers gripping hers. "You can do it if you try. Just hang on!"

She took short, sharp breaths and they hurt terribly. She grimaced with the effort. "Oh, it...hurts!" she moaned.

"I know. Oh, God, I know. But keep trying, Maggie. It'll get better. I promise."

So she kept trying, fading in and out of life until the sounds became familiar, until one day she opened her eyes and saw the white sheets and smelled the medicinal smell and saw sunlight filtered through the blinds across her bed.

Blinking, her lips raw, she looked up into a pale, haggard face with emerald green eyes and disheveled dark hair.

She frowned, numb from painkillers and sleep. "Hospital?" she managed weakly.

Clint drew a deep, heavy breath. "Hospital," he agreed. "Still hurt?"

She swallowed. "Could I...water?"

He got up from his chair and poured water and ice into a glass from the plastic pitcher by the bedside. He sat on the edge of the bed to lift her head so that she could sip the ice water.

"Oh, that's so good," she almost wept, "so good!"

"Your throat feels like sawdust, I imagine."

"Like...desert sand," she corrected, wincing as he laid her back on the pillows. "Am...am I broken somewhere?"

"A few ribs," he said.

The tone in his voice disturbed her. "What else?"

He ran a lean hand through his thick, dark hair. "You took a hell of a blow, Maggie," he said quietly.

"Clint, what else?" she cried.

"Your back, honey," he said gently.

With a feeling of horror she tried to move her legs...and couldn't.

"Oh, my God..." she whispered.

"Don't panic," Clint cautioned, brushing the damp hair away from her temples. "Don't panic. It isn't broken, just bruised. Your doctors say you'll be walking again in weeks."

Her eyes opened wide, searching his desperately. "You wouldn't...lie to me?"

His fingers brushed her cheek gently. "I'll never lie to you. It won't be easy, but you'll walk. All right?"

She relaxed. "All right."

"How did they...find you?" she asked.

A ghost of a smile touched his chiseled mouth. "Masterson's letter, in your purse.

It had your name and the ranch's address on it, remember?''

She nodded, toying with the sheet. ''I was…thinking about the cruise, when the car…''

''You might have told me where you were going,'' he remarked.

She flushed, turning her eyes away.

He drew a harsh breath. ''On second thought,'' he said gruffly, ''why the hell should you? God knows I didn't give you any reason to think I'd give a damn, did I, Maggie?''

She still couldn't answer him, the memories coming back full force now, hurting, hurting…!

''Don't,'' he said gently. ''Maggie, don't look back. It's going to take every ounce of strength you've got to get back on your feet. Don't waste it on me.''

She breathed unsteadily. ''You're right about that,'' she murmured tightly. ''It would be a waste.''

''I'm glad you agree,'' he replied, without a trace of emotion in his deep, slow voice.

She studied her pale hands. ''Why did you come?''

''Because Emma and Janna wouldn't rest until I did,'' he growled. ''Why else?''

''Well, I'll live,'' she said bitterly. ''And I'll walk. And I don't need any help from you, so why don't you go home?''

''Not without you.''

She gaped at him, but there was no hint of expression on his dark face.

''The minute I leave,'' he mused, ''you'd be up to your ears in self-pity.''

''I wouldn't either!''

He reached out and caught her cold, nervous fingers in his. ''I'll let you go the day you can walk away from me under your own power,'' he said. ''That ought to give you some incentive, hellcat.''

Hellcat. She remembered, without wanting to, the last time he'd called her that, pinning her down, holding her, hurting her, his hard mouth creating sensations that washed over her like fire.

"You're blushing, Maggie," he teased gently.

She jerked her hand away and her eyes with it. "I can go home...to the apartment," she faltered.

"Not on your life, honey," he said, and she recognized the willful, stubborn note in his voice. "Not if I have to tie you. Janna's home on vacation for the next three weeks, and I'll be damned if I'll leave you in an apartment alone and helpless."

"I'm not helpless!"

"No?" he taunted, his eyes sliding down her body.

She hit the covers with an impotent little fist. "I hate you!"

"As long as you're not indifferent," he chuckled. "Hatred can be exciting, little girl."

Her narrow, flashing pale eyes burned

into his. "Just you wait until I get back on my feet!"

He only smiled, leaning back in the chair, the tautness, the age draining out of him with the action. "I'll try, baby."

Something in the way he said it made her blush.

Time passed quickly after that. The pain lingered on for a few days, especially when they cut down on the painkillers, but Clint was always there, daring her to whimper about it. They gave her over to the physical therapists, and he was there too, watching, waiting, taunting. She worked twice as hard, focusing her weak muscles to do what she wanted them to, using the violent emotion she felt like a whip. She'd walk again. She would, if for no other reason than to prove to that jade-eyed devil she could!

Finally the day came when she was released from the hospital, when medical science had done all it could. She gazed over the back of the cab seat toward the

fading skyline of Miami as they reached
the airport. And she'd never even gotten
to see the cruise ship.

The flight home seemed to take no time
at all. Clint relaxed as he flew the small
single-engine plane, his eyes intent on the
controls and landmarks of small towns and
parks and farms and forests and herds of
cattle as they flew above the misty landscape.

She glanced at Clint. Did he really want
her to hate him, she wondered, or had he
only said it to irritate her? She remembered her own forwardness in her teens,
when she'd put him on a pedestal and done
everything but worship him. That must
have been unbearable for a man like Clint,
being followed around like a pet dog, as
he'd put it before she left the ranch.

Her eyes went back to the window,
glancing out at the wispy clouds. If only
she could live down that idiotic behavior,
if only she could wipe the slate clean between them and start over and be…friends.

The word almost choked her, but she realized belatedly that it was the only thing possible now. All the bridges were burned behind them. She'd done that all by herself.

Anyway, she thought with a chill, Lida would be back at the ranch waiting for him this time. She'd only seen the woman once, but that had been more than enough. It was going to make living at the ranch unbearable. It was why she'd fought so hard to go back to the apartment. But Clint, as usual, was going to have his way in spite of all her efforts to thwart him. Just like old times.

She stared down at her useless legs in the slacks she'd worn from Columbus on the bus. It seemed so long ago that Clint had swung her up behind him on the stallion.

It was the shock, the doctors had told her, that caused this temporary paralysis— the shock to her body, to her system, to her mind, and a good deal of bruising as well. At least she had the feeling back in them. But walking was going to be another matter altogether, and she shuddered mentally at what lay ahead. It was going to take a kind of determination she wasn't sure she possessed to make those muscles move again. What if she didn't have it? What if the doctors were wrong, and her spine had been damaged? What if...

"We're home!" Clint said above the engine noise, and nosed the small plane down toward the landing strip.

Janna met them with tears in her eyes, leaping from the big town car just as the propeller stopped spinning.

"Oh, Maggie, I'm so glad to see you," she wept, hugging her friend as though she'd come back from the dead instead of Miami.

Maggie forced herself to laugh as she patted Janna's shoulder. "I'm all right. I'm going to be fine. Ask Clint if you don't believe me. He insists!" she mumbled, glaring at him over Janna's shoulder.

He only grinned. "Move over, Janna, and let me get this load of potatoes in the car."

"I'm not a load of potatoes," Maggie protested as he slid his arms under and around her and carried her like a feather to the front seat of the car.

"You do have eyes," Janna remarked, tongue-in-cheek, as she opened the car door for Clint.

"And you do look fried," Clint seconded as he put her down gently on the seat. "Careful, Maggie, you'll singe yourself."

"You devil," she grumbled at him.

His eyes dropped deliberately to the soft curve of her mouth. "Daring me, honey?" he asked in a low voice as Janna went around the front of the car to get in.

"No!" she whispered back.

He smiled and closed the door. He went around the car, too, and opened the door on Janna. "Out," he said.

"But I can drive...!" she protested.

"Not my car, not with me in it. Out."

She gave a disgusted sigh and slid over next to Maggie. "I hate brothers," she muttered.

"That isn't what you always used to tell me," Maggie observed.

"Oh, do shut up," the younger girl moaned.

By night, Maggie was comfortably installed in the same guest bedroom she'd left, propped up with pillows, surrounded by books and magazines, pumped full of soup and sandwiches and hot coffee.

"But, Emma," she'd protested, "you'll spoil me."

"I'm just glad you're still around to be spoiled," came the reply as the housekeeper went out the door.

Janna sat down in the chair by the bed, laughing. "You might as well give up. You know that, don't you?"

Maggie smiled in surrender. "I ought to, I guess. Janna..."

"What?"

She looked down at her hands. "Is Lida here yet?"

Janna gaped at her. "What did you say?"

"Well...Clint said that Lida was coming back."

"The fool!" Janna got up and went to the window. A hard, angry sigh passed her lips. "He'll never learn, never! Why does he want her back here now, of all times? And when did he tell you she was coming?"

"Why...the Monday after I left here," she said.

"Well, she didn't show up. Thank God," Janna added angrily. "Hasn't he learned yet? My gosh, she went off and married that rich old man...is she leaving him already?"

"That's what Clint said."

"He'd be better off alone for the rest of his life. Oh, Maggie, why are men so stupid?" she moaned.

Maggie had to smile at the sincerity in her friend's soft voice. "I guess God made them that way so they'd be vulnerable to women."

"The only women my brother's vulnerable to are glorified streetwalkers," Janna grumbled. She eyed the oval face on the pillow with the cloudy tangle of wavy hair framing it. "Why hasn't he ever noticed you?"

Maggie reached for her coffee to try and keep Janna from seeing the color that surged in her cheeks. "I'm like his kid sister, you know that," she hedged.

"Well, it isn't due to a lack of effort on my part," Janna admitted. She sighed. "Well, can I get you anything?"

Maggie shook her head. "I'm spoiled enough, thanks. Don't let me keep you up. It's late."

Janna leaned down to hug her. "I'm so glad you're all right."

"So am I. I'm just sorry I missed the cruise. I would have enjoyed it so much…even if only because Duke wanted me to.''

Janna smiled. ''I liked that big man, too. Goodnight, my friend.''

''Goodnight.''

The door closed behind Janna, and the room seemed to shrink. She picked up a magazine and began to read, but the words blurred. With the silence and solitude, her mind began to work, weighing possibilities, worrying about her legs…

''So much for leaving you on your own,'' Clint said from the doorway, his eyes narrow as they studied her frowning face. ''Wallowing again?''

She made a face at him. ''I'm just reading this stupid magazine, is that all right?''

He folded his arms across his chest and leaned back against the door, just watching her. ''Were you reading? Or were you worrying?''

She sighed. ''Both.''

He moved forward, taking the magazine away. ''Lie down,'' he said, jerking a pillow from behind her head so that she could lie flat.

"You awful bully...!" she fussed.

"That and more. Here." He pulled up the covers and tucked them in around her chin. "Now go to sleep and stop torturing yourself. All you have to remember is that you're going to walk again."

Her eyes, wide and a little frightened, looked up into his. "I will, won't I, Clint?" she asked softly, letting the barriers down just long enough to seek reassurance.

"Yes," he said quietly, and with certainty.

She relaxed against the pillows. "Is...is Lida coming soon?" she murmured, avoiding his eyes.

"Lida?"

"Yes. You know, you said..."

"God, I forgot," he said heavily. "She called just after I left for Miami and gave Emma some spiel about changing her mind and going to Majorca instead. It didn't even register at the time Emma told me." His jade eyes glared down at her. "You've given me a hell of a bad time, Irish."

"Sorry," she said softly.

"Show me," he murmured deeply, bending to her mouth.

She stared at him, shaken, not knowing how to take this gentle assault, not knowing if she dared to take him seriously.

His long finger traced the soft tremulous curve of her mouth. "You don't trust me, do you?" he asked quietly.

She shook her head. Without words, her eyes showed the hurt, the memory of why she'd left here.

He tilted her face just a little and his mouth brushed against hers softly, slowly, in a kiss so tender, so exquisitely caring that it brought tears misting into her eyes.

He drew back and searched her face with darkening, intense eyes. "I've got a hard head," he murmured absently, "and sometimes it takes a hell of a knock to get through to me. But I learn fast, little girl, and I don't make the same mistakes twice.''

She lowered her eyes as the words got through to her. He meant that he wasn't playing any more, that he wasn't going to encourage her to lose her head. It should have made her happy. Instead, there was a king-sized lump in her throat.

''I'm...I'm so tired, Clint,'' she murmured.

''No doubt.'' He smoothed her hair with a gentle hand. ''I'm safe, Maggie. I'm not going for your throat any more. We'll keep things at a friendly level from now on. Is that what you want?''

''Oh, yes,'' she breathed, and didn't look up in time to see the tiny flinch of his eyelids.

''Sleep well,'' he said in a strange tone, and tugging playfully at a strand of her hair, he turned and left her there.

She snuggled down into the pillows. At least, she thought miserably, they'd be friends for once in their lives. Maybe that would ease the hurt a little. And maybe all wolves would suddenly become vegetarians.

Nine

"Is that the best you can do, Irish?" Clint taunted as she pulled herself along the parallel bars in the makeshift gym he'd had equipped for her.

She glared at him, painstakingly dragging her weak legs along behind her as she let her arms take her weight. "You try it!" she panted. "Do you think you could do any better?"

"Sure," he chuckled.

She stopped to catch her breath. "You," she told him, "are a slave driver."

"I'll have you back on your feet in two more weeks," he said smugly. "If," he added darkly, "you stop cheating. Use your legs, Maggie, not your arms. Stand up, dammit!"

Her lower lip trembled. Tears formed in her eyes. "Don't you think I'm trying to?" she cried.

He came forward, lifting her up in his arms like a tearful child. He carried her to an armchair by the window and sank down in it, holding her on his lap until the cloudburst was past. He passed a handkerchief into her hand and sat back, watching her mop and sniff away the evidence.

"I'm sorry," she mumbled.

"You're human," he told her. "So am I, although I don't think you like to believe it. I don't want to browbeat you, but you'll never get on your feet again unless you try to walk. Dragging won't cut it, baby."

She thumped her small fist against his broad chest under the deep gray shirt. "I'm trying!"

"Try harder."

She glared at him with all the pent-up rage she felt. "I'd like to hit you!" she said hotly.

His eyes narrowed. "All that sweet, wild emotion," he whispered, "and no way to let it out, is that it? Let me help you..."

He caught her face in both hands and brought it up to his mouth, kissing her suddenly, violently, with a force that made her clutch at his shoulders to steady herself. She felt the wildness in her own blood reaching out to him, burning him back, in a release that was better than tears. With a hard moan, her arms went around his neck, her mouth opened hungrily under his, and she gave him back the kiss with every bit of strength in her body and all the longing she had felt for him since her teens.

Suddenly he drew away, his eyes burning, his breath jerking as he managed to catch it. "My God," he breathed unsteadily, and his hands bit into her upper arms like steel clasps. "What are you trying to do to me?"

Dazed, vaguely embarrassed at her passionate response, she dragged her eyes down to the hard pulse at his brown throat. "You…started it," she accused shakily.

"It's all I can do to keep from finishing it, you little fool," he said deeply. He stood up abruptly, met her eyes as he placed her hands on the bars, probing them in a silence that simmered between them.

"The sooner I get you out of here, the better," he said in a goaded tone. "Now, stand up, dammit!"

Whipped by the anger in his voice, the admission that he wanted to be rid of her, she forced her body to go erect, forced the screaming muscles in her legs to move.

"I'm going to walk if it kills me," she told him.

"Don't tell me," he replied. "Show me."

"Stand back and watch, then." And she moved her legs, for the first time.

From that first step, it was on to a second, a third, and finally as many as it took to go the length of the parallel bars. It was the greatest feeling of accomplishment Maggie had ever known, and better than any medicine. She could walk again. She could walk alone. She could walk away from Clint for good.

Not that it seemed to bother Clint. Once he had her moving alone, he seemed to vanish, leaving her with Emma and Janna for moral support while he went about his business. He kept his distance except at meals, and then he made sure the conversation was kept on general topics. To Maggie he was courteous and polite, nothing more. It was worse than the old days, when he fought with her. It hurt.

Janna was sitting with her one night, when Clint passed by the open door with little more than a glance and a nod. Maggie muttered something under her breath and Janna got up and closed the door.

She turned, eyeing Maggie curiously. "Do you hate him so much?" she asked gently.

Maggie pushed a strand of hair out of her eyes. "I'm indifferent," she lied. "Numb, I guess. I don't think there's enough emotion left in me for hate."

"Serves him right, I guess." The smaller girl sighed. "All the hearts he's broken over the years, it was poetic justice."

Maggie's heart jumped and ran away, but the excitement never touched her composed expression. "What do you mean?"

"If you'd seen his face when he got that call about the accident you were in, you wouldn't have to ask." Janna sighed as she sank back down in the chair by Maggie's bed. "He went whiter than any sheet. I've never seen anything upset Clint like that, not in all my life. He went straight to the airstrip without even packing. And when he got to Miami, he never left you except to sleep, and not for long at that.'' Janna studied her fingernails. ''The doctors told him you weren't going to make it, that you weren't trying to live. He wouldn't accept that. He sat and held your hand and talked to you...I stayed for two days, then he made me come home when he saw you were going to be all right.'' She smiled. ''He said somebody had to run the ranch while he was gone.''

Maggie stared at her for a long time before she spoke. ''I don't remember anything....'' She sighed. ''Oh, Janna, I'm so sorry I worried everyone. It was such a stupid...''

''It could have happened to any of us. All I wanted to do was make you understand that Clint cares.''

Maggie smiled wistfully. ''It's guilt, Janna, not caring,'' she corrected gently. ''He...he said some very cruel things to me the night before I left the ranch for

Miami. I don't think either one of us will ever forget. God help me," she said, her eyes closing on the memories, "I don't think I can forget or forgive him, ever, for what he did to me that night."

There was such a deathly silence in the room that Maggie quickly opened her eyes—and found Clint standing just inside the door, his face frozen, his gaze dark and quiet and faintly violent. That he'd heard those words was evident.

"I wanted to remind you that Jones is bringing that bull tomorrow morning," Clint told Janna, without bothering to spare Maggie another glance. "I've got a meeting in Atlanta, so I won't be back until late. Have the boys put him in that new pen and get the vet out here."

"I will," Janna said uncomfortably. "Are you going in the morning?"

He nodded. "Goodnight."

He was gone, and Janna met Maggie's wounded eyes in the silence that followed.

"Maggie, what happened?" she asked gently.

But Maggie shook her head with a tearful smile. It didn't bear telling. Not to anyone.

It was late, and the house was long asleep, but Maggie couldn't even close her eyes. With a quiet sigh, she finally gave up and got out of bed, painstakingly pulling on her long jade green robe and making her way into the dark hall and down the stairs.

Her legs were still sluggish, but by taking her time, she made it to the kitchen without stumbling. A cup of hot chocolate, she thought, just might put her to sleep. Failing that, she was ready to try a sledgehammer.

While the milk was heating, she got down a heavy mug and filled it sparingly with a tablespoon of sugar and one of cocoa. And all the while, she hated her own tongue for the words Clint had heard. After everything he'd done for her, and she had to throw it out like that, and he had to hear it. Her eyes closed on the pain. And she hadn't really meant it at all.

She poured the hot milk into the mug on top of the sugar and cocoa. The sudden opening of the door startled her so that she almost dropped the pot. She whirled to find Clint standing just inside the doorway.

"What the hell do you think you're doing?" he asked quietly. His dark hair was rumpled, his shirt half undone, his dark face heavily lined as if he'd tried to sleep and couldn't.

"I...just wanted to have a cup of hot chocolate," she murmured, as she placed the pot in the sink and ran water in it.

"Who told you to get out of bed and start climbing up and down stairs in the dark?" he persisted.

She flashed a glance at him. "The President, both houses of Congress and my senator," she said with a hint of her old spirit.

"You left out your representative," he mused, and for just an instant a smile touched his hard mouth. "You ought to be in bed, honey."

Amazing what the soft endearment could do to her nerves, she thought, sitting quickly down at the table in front of her hot chocolate before her legs gave way. "I'll go back up in just a minute."

"Stubborn little mule," he accused. "All right, I'll have a glass of tea and wait for you. How about some cheese and bread?"

Her eyebrows went up. "Hoop cheese?" she asked hopefully.

"If I can find where Emma hides it. Aha!" He pulled it out of the refrigerator, sliced some of it, and put it on a saucer. "Would you rather have crackers or bread?"

"Crackers!"

He laughed softly as he poured himself a glass of tea and plopped ice cubes into it. "Same here."

Seconds later, he put the cheese and crackers on the table between them and relaxed in the chair next to hers, drinking his tea thirstily.

"Couldn't you sleep?" she asked, suddenly shy of him.

"No," he replied quietly.

She shrugged. "Neither could I." She munched on a piece of cheese.

He finished off his part of the cheese and crackers and leaned back in his chair to study her. "Look at me," he said suddenly.

She met his level gaze, startled, and as quickly looked away from it.

"The robe matches your eyes," he remarked.

She smiled. "That's why Janna gave it to me, or so she said."

"Legs hurt?" he asked.

She shook her head. "I took my time coming down the steps. After all," she reminded him, "you were the one who said I needed more exercise."

He drained his glass. "I said too damned much," he replied. "Hurry up, honey, I'm not leaving you down here alone."

She finished her hot chocolate and got up to put the cup in the sink. As she turned away from the sink, she found herself being lifted into a pair of steely, warm arms and carried out of the kitchen.

"Oh, don't," she protested gently, pushing at his shoulder. "Clint, I'm too heavy...!"

He flicked off the light switch in the kitchen as he carried her out into the hall and up the staircase. His eyes, dark and strange, looked deep into hers. "You don't weigh anything, little girl. It's like carrying an armload of soft, warm velvet."

"If you're going to make fun of me, just put me down and I'll walk!" she said defensively, stirred by the sensations being this close to him was causing.

"Oh, hell no, you won't," he replied

imperturbably, and tightened his hold on her.

"You awful bully!"

"You little shrew."

She drew a deep, hard breath and glared up at him with her green eyes blazing. "It's like arguing with a stone wall!" she growled.

He chuckled softly. "See how simple life is when you stop struggling, Irish?"

Her lips pursed in a sulking pout. "I won't even dignify that remark with an answer."

"You'd hate it if you could fight me and win, Irish," he said gently.

She lowered her eyes to his open collar, where the bronzed flesh with its covering of dark hair was tantalizingly visible. She could feel the hardness of that broad chest where she was pressed against it, and she wanted suddenly to reach out and touch that warm rough skin. A tremor went lightly through her body.

He looked down when he felt it and

caught her eyes, held them, and searched them with an intensity that made her heart race.

He drew a deep, harsh breath and kept walking. He carried her into her room and laid her on the bed as quickly as if she'd been an armload of burning straw.

"This time, stay put," he growled, and his eyes were blazing as they looked down into hers.

She glared up at him. Her breath came in irregular gasps, from the proximity she'd endured, from the hunger of loving him. "Must you always growl at me?" she whispered.

"Do you have to be told what I'd rather do?" he asked flatly, and his eyes slid over her like a warm caress, from her lovely flushed face in its wild tangle of dark, wavy long hair down to her slender body. "I want you to the point where it's like having an arm cut off, does that make you feel better, hellcat?" he asked harshly.

The admission stunned her. He'd said

something like that before, but she always thought it was part of the humiliation he'd thrown at her. She lay there quietly, staring up at him like a curious young cat, her eyes asking questions as they met his.

"That's all you know anything about—wanting," she said quietly, her eyes accusing.

"What should I believe in?" he asked. "Love? It's a myth, little girl. An illusion that doesn't last past the marriage vows."

"How do you know?"

He studied her mouth with a mocking smile. "How do you?" He bent forward, leaning on the arms that pinioned her on either side. "I've always been able to read you like a book," he murmured, holding her eyes. "No, I'm not guilt-ridden, and don't you believe that I am. There are a thousand reasons why I came to Miami after you, but guilt wasn't one of them."

She stared up at him, curious but afraid to voice the question.

"You know one of them," he whispered deeply, studying her mouth. "But I'm not going to offer you marriage, Maggie. Not now, not ever."

She swallowed nervously. "I won't be your mistress," she said unsteadily. "I won't, Clint."

"Could you feel with another man what you feel with me?" he challenged roughly.

She shifted restlessly on the pillow. "There are other things."

"Name one."

"Children!" she shot at him, feeling vulnerable under those cutting green eyes.

Something came and went in his face. He studied her for a long time before he spoke, weighing what she'd said with the soft light in her eyes.

"You want children?" he said.

"Of course."

"There's not any 'of course' about it, little girl," he said solemnly. "Lida couldn't bear the thought of them. I can't remember another woman I've been around who even considered them as part of a relationship."

"That doesn't come as any surprise to me," she said flatly.

He ignored the sarcasm. "Do you know, Maggie," he told her gently, "I've never thought about children?"

She toyed with the pillowcase. "Why should you?" she murmured. "You don't need anybody. You never have."

His fingers tugged hers away from the pillowcase to swallow them gently, firmly. "I'm human," he said, his face solemn. "We all need someone from time to time, Maggie."

"I can't picture you being lonely," she murmured. "What with all the women following you around like..." She was going to say pet dogs, but with the memory came pain and her face went white.

"Don't, for God's sake!" he growled huskily. He slid his hands under her and lifted her up against his hard, warm chest, rocking her gently, his face buried in her dark hair, his hand tangling in the smoky tresses so hard it hurt.

"Clint, I want to go home," she whispered shakily, her eyes closing as she yielded against him, glorying in the feel of him, the tangy scent of his cologne mingling with the spicy soap he used.

"Why?" he asked at her ear.

"Because I've got to find a job," she said weakly. "I can't stay here..." It was hard to think this close to him. She remembered too well the feel of his hard mouth against her own, and she wanted it so... Her nails bit into his shoulders involuntarily as she fought to keep that hunger from being betrayed by her own body.

"Stay with me," he whispered softly, and she felt his lips moving in her hair, against her cheek, the corner of her mouth. His hands came up to cup her face and hold it up to his narrow, glittering eyes. "Be my woman, Maggie."

Her lips trembled as they formed an answer, but his mouth whispered across them, his tongue tracing gently the soft curve of her upper lip. "I like the way you taste, Margaretta Leigh," he murmured sensuously.

"You...you just like women," she whispered unsteadily, and tried to draw back.

"Honey, I don't want anybody else," he said matter-of-factly. "I haven't for a long time."

She couldn't find a way to answer him, and that seemed to amuse him. He watched her with eyes that were as patient as they were calculating.

"Caught in my own web," he mused, and mischief danced in his dark green eyes. "Doomed to a lifetime of frustrated desire for the one woman I can't have. My God, I wonder if I'm too old for the French Foreign Legion?"

Her eyes lit up. She laughed, her eyes glowing like liquid emeralds, her face flushed and soft and radiant with laughter, her hair like a dark halo framing her face.

Clint caught his breath at the picture she
made, at the color and animation in that
sad little face.

"Think it's funny, do you?" he growled
in mock anger, roughly cradling her
against him. He bent and kissed her sav-
agely, his mouth demanding and getting a
response from her lips. He drew back just
far enough to see the eagerness in her eyes.
"Now laugh, hellcat," he murmured
deeply.

She reached up and touched his mouth
with slender, cool fingers. "Barbarian,"
she whispered.

He smiled. "Did you like it?" he
taunted.

She dragged her eyes down to his brown
neck. "A lady never admits such things."

"Lady, hell." He brought her mouth up
to his and cherished it softly, slowly, with
such tender ardor that she gasped. "You're
a woman," he whispered huskily. "All
woman. My woman. You belong to me,
little cat."

She pushed against his chest and sank down on the pillows with a wistful sigh. "No," she told him quietly, and tears brightened her sad eyes. "Not that way."

He drew a deep, short breath and stood up, moving away from the bed to light a cigarette. He took a long draw before he spoke. "Is that final, Maggie?" he asked.

"Yes," she whispered. "I'm sorry."

"The world's full of women, Maggie." He laughed shortly, and threw a mocking glance at her just before he left the room.

Clint was already gone when she got downstairs the next morning. Janna was waiting for her at the table.

"It's about time," she teased. "I thought you were going to sleep all day."

"I thought about it," Maggie replied with a wan smile. She pushed away the plate at her place, ignored the bacon and scrambled eggs and toast on the table, and settled for a cup of black coffee.

"Okay, you might as well tell me what

happened," Janna grumbled. "Clint did the same thing. He wouldn't eat in spite of all Emma's coaxing, and he looked like a thundercloud when he went out the door. Was it another argument?"

Maggie lowered her eyes to the reflection of the light in her coffee. "You might say that."

"It's like trying to coax a clam open. Maggie…!"

"He wants me to be his mistress," she replied impatiently, meeting Janna's gaping stare calmly. "And I said no. That's all."

"That's all, she says!" Janna gasped. "You mean you finally stopped fighting long enough to get involved with each other!"

"We're not…involved. At least, not that way." Maggie sipped her coffee. Tears formed in her eyes and she bit at her lip to keep them from falling, but she felt the betraying trickle down her face. "Oh,

Janna, what am I going to do?'' she whispered brokenly. "I love him so!"

Janna got to her feet and wrapped her thin arms around the older girl, hugging her quietly until the flood of tears showed signs of slowing.

"I'm sorry," Janna murmured. "I feel responsible, sending you down here when you didn't want to come. Oh, Maggie, why didn't you tell me?" she wailed. "I'd never have insisted…!"

"It's all right, it's not your fault," she replied soothingly. "You can't help it that you've got a hardheaded, half-savage beast for a brother. I just don't understand why…. One day he'd tease me, the next he'd kiss me, the next he'd act as if he hated me… Oh, Janna, I'm so confused."

"He wants you," Janna said, with an ear-to-ear grin.

"Of course he wants me, for all that he spent the first week I was here denying it," she sighed, wiping at her red eyes. "But that's all there is. He told me that he didn't even believe in love, Janna, and that he'd never marry. He wants me, but I can't settle for that kind of relationship. As much as I love him, I can't.''

"He wanted Lida, you know," the younger girl reminded her gently. "But he wouldn't have rushed to her bedside, or spent weeks helping her to walk again."

"Wouldn't he?" Maggie asked wistfully. "How do you know that? No," she shook her head. "It's only a physical kind of caring that he feels for me. And it's not enough."

Janna nodded miserably. "What will you do?"

"What can I do? I'll go home." She finished her coffee. "Temporarily, at least. Janna, don't look like that," she pleaded when she saw the crestfallen expression on her friend's face. "You know I wouldn't be able to bear it. He'd call you, like he always has. When he comes to town, he'll come to see you. Do you think I could bear that?"

"How will I bear being without you?" Janna murmured unsteadily. "All these years, and growing up together, and sharing the apartment... Oh, Maggie, I'll go with you!"

"You haven't heard a word I've said," Maggie groaned.

Janna sighed. "Yes, I have. Oh, darn Clint, anyway! Why did he have to bring things to a head? You could have gone on hating each other for years!"

That brought a smile to the pale green eyes. "Oh, Janna, you're so comforting!" she laughed weakly. "Come on up and help me pack. I want to be long gone when Clint gets back."

"I'll go with you!"

"You will not. You're on vacation, and he is your brother," she said firmly. "Besides, isn't your mother due home soon?"

"Yes," came the grudging reply.

"Then that's settled. Everything will work out," she added gently. "I promise you, everything will work out. Now stop pouting and come help me pack.''

Atlanta was exciting and new, and Maggie's job with a firm of corporation lawyers kept her energies focussed on coping with a different routine.

Day by day it was getting easier to let the past rest. Janna had argued, when she returned from vacation, that if Maggie would just give it a little time, everything would be different. But Maggie was adamant. She'd already found a job, and an apartment downtown, and was in the process of moving when Janna walked in the door.

''He's changed, you know,'' Janna told her quietly during a lull in packing. ''When he isn't working himself into a coma, he just…sits. Mama came home and even *she* couldn't get through to him. It's like he's…grieving.''

''For me?'' Maggie scoffed. ''That'll be the day. If anything, he was glad to see the last of me. All I ever did was irritate him.''

"Are you really over him, already?" Janna asked quietly.

Maggie turned away and went back to the mountain of clothes she'd stacked on her bed. "Sit down and let me tell you all about my new job!" she said brightly.

One of her new bosses was young and single, and he reminded her vaguely of Brent. They seemed to gravitate together, and it was no time before she was going out with him. But with the understanding that it was going to be strictly a friendship on her part.

"That suits me." Jack Kasey grinned from his superior height. "Even though she can't marry me, Sophia Loren gets so *jealous*!"

"Are you sane?" Maggie teased.

He tossed his blond head arrogantly. "Madam, how dare you?" he demanded.

"Well, excuse me!"

"I should think so!" he replied, unruffled. He reached in his pocket and held out his hand, palm up. There was nothing in it. "Want one?" he asked.

"One what?" She blinked.

"Funny, that's just what my psychiatrist always asks."

"Oh, good heavens," she laughed. "You're the living end!"

"But of course! And I'm loaded, too," he said in a stage whisper. "How about a steak tomorrow night?"

"I'd love it!"

"Great. I know this little restaurant..."

After the little restaurant, there was another little disco place, and then an all-night bar. It was after two o'clock in the morning when she got back to her apartment.

"Sorry to keep you up so late," Jack apologized as he walked with her from the elevator to her apartment door. "Next time, I'll try to remember that we're both working stiffs."

"I enjoyed it, though," she said, laughing.

"So did I." He grinned. "Well, good-night, fair lady, my dragon awaits without."

"Don't ride him too hard, now," she cautioned. "You know how nasty dragons can get when they're overworked!"

"I'll remember!" he called as the elevator door shut.

With a sigh, she fit her key into the lock and walked in. There was a light on in the living room, and she hadn't remembered leaving it on. The carpet muffled her footsteps as she moved cautiously forward. The lock was strong, surely no thief had been able to...

She came silently to the doorway and froze there. Clint was sitting in an armchair facing the hall, his eyes quiet and dark in the distance, his face solemn.

"Wha...how...how did you get in here?" she asked hoarsely.

"Never mind how," he said in a voice tight with anger. "Who the hell were you with, and where have you been half the night?''

She threw her evening bag down on the coffee table and glared at him, the color of her emerald green dress making her eyes even more vivid.

''None of your business, Clint,'' she replied with a calm she was far from feeling. ''I don't owe you any answers.''

He lit a cigarette, his eyes never leaving hers. ''I asked you a question. I can get an answer in any number of ways. One,'' he remarked quietly, ''would be to lay you out on that sofa.''

She flushed at the insinuation. ''I thought you were tired of giving me lessons,'' she said tightly.

He started to get up.

''All right!'' she said quickly. ''I...I was out with one of the lawyers in the firm I work for. Just...just a friendly date, Clint. He's very much like Brent.''

He sank back against the cushion, with a heavy sigh. ''Maggie, is that the kind of man who really appeals to you?'' he asked wearily.

She studied her evening shoes. ''What kind of man are you talking about?''

''Clowns. Boys.''

''They don't make demands,'' she said on a sigh.

''No,'' he agreed. ''They don't. Why are you afraid of a man who would? Do you feel that inadequate, little girl?''

''Yes,'' she said, in what was little more than a whisper.

''Why?''

She shook her head and perched on the arm of the sofa, her eyes avoiding his.

She heard him get up, heard the muffled thud of his footsteps as he came to her. His lean hands caught her shoulders and forced her to look up at him.

''Because of what that excuse for a fiancé said to you?'' he asked quietly. ''Or because of what I did to you?''

''A little of…both,'' she murmured, hating the weakness he could cause with only an impersonal touch like this.

He let her go and moved away, smoking his cigarette quietly, standing in front of the window to watch with blank eyes the colorful glow of the city stretching to the horizon.

"Please," she murmured, "why are you here? Is everyone all right at home...?"

"Everyone," he agreed wearily. "Except me."

She studied his straight back. "What's wrong?" she asked gently.

"I love you, Maggie."

She felt the words. Actually felt them, like a blinding surge of electric current that made her tremble.

He turned, and she saw the truth in his eyes, in the deep lines of his face.

"Have I shocked you?" he asked harshly. "God knows, I've shocked myself. I didn't think I could feel that for a woman. I didn't think I was capable of it." He took a long draw from his cigarette, and his eyes gazed at every inch of her from head to toe. "Do you want to know what it felt like when you left? Do you want to know how many nights I've spent sitting in the chair by my bed staring out into the darkness, missing you? My God, I have hurt until it feels like I've been cut in two."

Her lips parted tremulously, but she couldn't speak. It was too new, too incredible. Was she asleep and dreaming it all?

He put out the cigarette and came toward her like a cat, all muscle and grace and vibrant masculinity. He reached down and swung her up into his arms.

"You don't believe me, do you?" he asked quietly. "Let me prove it to you, Margaretta Leigh. Let me show you what I feel."

His arms brought her sensuously close and his mouth burned down into hers, opening it, tasting it, devouring it with a hunger that was fierce and blistering.

He dropped down onto the couch, hold-

ing her across his lap, touching every soft
line of her face with his lips, tenderly
smoothing away the tears that his gentle-
ness brought from her closed eyes.

"Clint…!" she whispered brokenly,
clinging to him.

"What do you feel, when I kiss you?"
he asked against her soft mouth, his breath
coming quick and heavy.

"As if I'm…being burned…alive," she
wept, and her fingers went trembling to his
cheek, the silvery hair at his temples. "I
love you so much," she breathed. "I love
you so…!"

"Show me," he challenged, bending his
head. "Sweet little enemy, show me how
much!"

She brought her mouth down onto his
and kissed him slowly, hungrily, her nails
digging into his back, her lips parting sensuously under his.

He drew back a breath, his eyes almost
black with what he was feeling, his heavy
heartbeat shaking her. He studied her

flushed face, her misty, yielding eyes, and with a tender deliberation, his lean hand slid up her body over the soft, young curves until he felt her tremble.

"Do you like this?" he whispered gently.

She nodded, choked with the force of her own emotions so that even a word was impossible.

"So do I, little innocent," he said tenderly. He bent and kissed her gently, and his lips curved in a smile against the soft moan that broke from her throat as his hand moved again.

Her head fell back into the crook of his arm and she looked up at him with eyes that held all of heaven.

"I've fought this until I thought it was going to kill me," he said, and she could see the seriousness in his eyes. "Honey, I want more from you than a night in my bed. I want children with you. I want to be there when you hurt so I can hold you until the tears go away. I want to stand between you and the world and keep you safe. God, Maggie, I can't bear to live without you!'' he whispered torturously. ''Marry me, Irish. Live with me. Love me.''

Tears were flowing down her cheeks. ''Yes,'' she whispered, and found herself drowning in his ardor almost before she could get the word out.

Minutes later, he tore himself away from her and stood up, smoothing his ruffled hair, fastening the buttons of his shirt.

''We'd better settle for a civil ceremony,'' he said huskily, ''and soon.''

She nodded, straightening her clothes and her hair while her heart threatened to storm through her chest.

''When did you know?'' she asked, moving into the kitchen and starting a pot of coffee.

He stood in the doorway watching her with a smoking cigarette in his hand, looking so attractive, it took all her willpower not to throw herself at him.

"The summer you were seventeen," he said gently, smiling.

She gaped at him.

"I wanted you," he said. "I couldn't get you away from the ranch fast enough, I wanted you so. From that day on, it was a losing battle. I used every excuse I could think of to keep you away from the ranch, to avoid you when you were there. My God, I'd never felt like that about a woman, any woman. And you were little more than a child." He shook his head with a wistful sigh. "I thought it would eventually go away. Right up to the day you called and told Emma you were engaged." He laughed shortly. "I went into a black sulk for days. I got drunk out of my mind. Two of my men threatened to quit because I rode them so hard. And nobody knew why, except me. But even then I wouldn't admit it."

"And then I came for the summer," she said.

"And I went over the edge." He

reached out and touched her cheek. "Oh, baby, you'll never know how I fought to keep my hands off you. Until that day by the stream, when I finally let myself go…and every second of it was like a dark, heady wine. If you'd touched me the way I wanted you to…" He broke off with a deep, short breath. "I tried to stay away from you, and it got harder all the time. That last night…it was either make you hate me or carry you upstairs. I hated what I did, even while I was doing it. But at that time, I still didn't think I wanted marriage." His eyes closed. "I found out how much I wanted it when they called me from Miami. I damned near crashed the plane getting to you, and I swore if you made it I wouldn't waste a day getting you to the altar. Then you started recovering and when you remembered what I'd done, you hated me. I couldn't seem to get close to you again until we had that midnight snack in the kitchen. That was another close call. And then I began to have doubts all over again. I knew you wanted me. But I wasn't sure you loved me. You'd been infatuated with me for so long, I couldn't be sure...in a way, I was testing you that night. If I'd been able to make you say yes with no offer of marriage...I thought it would prove that you really did love me. But you said no. And I got my back up and left without saying goodbye. Then you left, and I was too damned proud to go after you."

She met his eyes and smiled. "Why did you come tonight?"

His finger traced her mouth. "Because Janna told me you loved me," he said softly, "and put me out of my misery."

She moved into his arms and pressed close. Her eyes closed as he drew her up against him.

"Are...are you sure you want to marry me?" she asked.

He chuckled deeply. "I don't see any alternatives. We can't very well have a family any other way."

"I hope they're all boys, and they look just like you."

"I want one little girl with dark hair and green eyes."

Her lips brushed his chin. "I'll see what I can do."

He kissed her gently. "Let's call Janna," he said with a grin. "And mother. And especially," he added with a glint in his eyes, "Brent."

"You were jealous!" she gasped.

"Hell, yes! And angry. He kept getting in my way. That night in the pool... Oh, that night," he whispered against her mouth, "Maggie, I could feel your hands on me for days, do you know that? That was when I began to suspect what I really felt."

She toyed with a button on his shirt. "Does that mean," she asked, "that I can't tie ribbons on the cows' tails anymore?"

He glared down at her. "Maggie..." he began warningly.

She reached up and linked her arms around his neck. "Let's call Janna," she murmured contentedly, "and tell her we've decided to become very friendly enemies."

He smiled down into her eyes. "Sweet enemy," he whispered, "show me how friendly you want to be."

And she did.

*   *   *   *   *

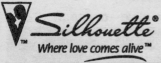

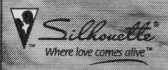